PRAISE FOR
QUEER MYTHOLOGY

ᖇᖶ

"Fascinating and validating, these mythological heroes are highlighted with great care and exquisite art."

—SARA FARIZAN, AWARD-WINNING AUTHOR OF
IF YOU COULD BE MINE AND *DEAD FLIP*

"Guido A. Sanchez has created a lovely collection of inclusive and affirming myths from around the world that show that queer folks have always been here, and we have always been heroes."

—CARRIE HARRIS, AUTHOR OF *XAVIER'S INSTITUTE:
LIBERTY & JUSTICE FOR ALL*

"Dive into the rich tapestry of mythology through a queer lens with Guido A. Sanchez, as he unveils hidden stories, celebrates overlooked characters, and redefines the boundaries of traditional narratives in his groundbreaking book, *Queer Mythology*. Drawing upon a deep well of cultural and historical knowledge, Sanchez skillfully weaves together a collection of myths and legends from around the world, shedding light on the often-neglected tales with truth and the underlining message we queer folx need to hear: We've always existed."

—DAMIEN ALAN LOPEZ, AWARD-WINNING
AUTHOR OF *I AM A PRINCE*

"I went through such a range of emotions reading these beautiful stories. While I thoroughly enjoyed each one, I couldn't help but wonder how many more stories about our LGBTQIA+ community have been lost, either intentionally or not, and that made me a little sad and angry. But the emotion I settled on was gratitude. I'm grateful that so many of these tales have been found and retold so they can be shared once more, letting the world know not only that we're still here, but that we always have been."

—JAYE MCBRIDE, WRITER AND COMEDIAN

"With each story in *Queer Mythology,* Guido A. Sanchez gives each reader a chance to see themselves reflected, proving that queer stories and people have always existed and have always been part of the narrative. An important, fun, and relatable book of tales that should be part of every kid's introduction into mythology."

"*Queer Mythology* retells timeless fables from around the world to reveal their queer truth. Pitched just right for middle-grade readers, these epic tales are perfectly complemented by the gorgeous illustrations. I was reminded of all of our queer ancestors, both real and imaginary, and how much they want all young LGBTQIA+ people to find joy. The legends in *Queer Mythology* are truly compelling."

"Positive and upbeat, much needed and highly readable, *Queer Mythology* is an invitation for readers young and old to consider our world through a more inclusive lens. Read it, share it, and enjoy!"

"You may think you know what the tracks on this album are going to be, but Guido A. Sanchez surprises, not only with some deep cuts drawn from a wide array of world mythologies, but also with some golden oldies, now with all their original queerness intact. A great addition to the collections of mythology-lovers everywhere and an important reminder that LGBTQIA+ heroes have been with us all along—we just didn't always get to hear their stories fully told. Until now."

"*Queer Mythology* is a definitive tome, as each page is brimming of wonder and inspiration. It's a testament to the power of storytelling, and what it can mean to us as queer people."

Queer Mythology

EPIC LEGENDS FROM AROUND THE WORLD

GUIDO A. SANCHEZ

Illustrated by JAMES FENNER

RP | TEENS
PHILADELPHIA

Running Press Teens
Hachette Book Group
1290 Avenue of the Americas, New York, NY 10104
www.runningpress.com/rpkids
@runningpresskids

First Edition: October 2024

Published by Running Press Teens, an imprint of Hachette Book Group, Inc.
The Running Press Teens name and logo are trademarks of Hachette Book Group, Inc.

The Hachette Speakers Bureau provides a wide range of authors for speaking events.
To find out more, go to www.hachettespeakersbureau.com or email
HachetteSpeakers@hbgusa.com.

Running Press books may be purchased in bulk for business, educational, or promotional use.
For more information, please contact your local bookseller or the Hachette Book Group Special
Markets Department at Special.Markets@hbgusa.com.

The publisher is not responsible for websites (or their content) that are not owned by the publisher.

Print book cover and interior design by Mary Boyer

Library of Congress Cataloging-in-Publication Data
Names: Sanchez, Guido A., author. | Fenner, James (Illustrator), illustrator.
Title: Queer mythology : epic legends from around the world / Guido A. Sanchez ;
illustrated by James Fenner.
Description: First edition. | Philadelphia : RP | Teens, [2024] |
Audience: Ages 11 and up | Audience: Grades 7-9
Identifiers: LCCN 2023054412 (print) | LCCN 2023054413 (ebook) |
ISBN 9780762487202 (hardcover) | ISBN 9780762487219 (ebook)
Subjects: LCSH: Sexual minorities—Folklore—Juvenile literature. |
Sexual minorities in literature—Juvenile literature.
Classification: LCC HQ76.26 .S36 2024 (print) | LCC HQ76.26 (ebook) |
DDC 306.76/6—dc23/eng/20240102
LC record available at https://lccn.loc.gov/2023054412
LC ebook record available at https://lccn.loc.gov/2023054413

ISBNs: 978-0-7624-8720-2 (hardcover), 978-0-7624-8721-9 (ebook)

Printed in Dongguan, China

APS

10 9 8 7 6 5 4 3 2 1

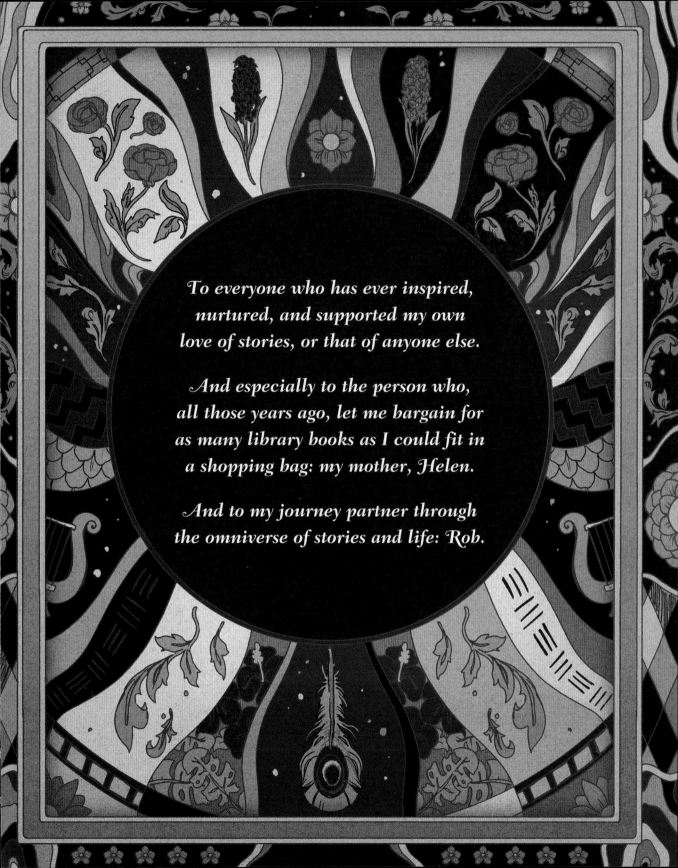

To everyone who has ever inspired,
nurtured, and supported my own
love of stories, or that of anyone else.

And especially to the person who,
all those years ago, let me bargain for
as many library books as I could fit in
a shopping bag: my mother, Helen.

And to my journey partner through
the omniverse of stories and life: Rob.

CONTENTS

WE HAVE ALWAYS EXISTED

AN INTRODUCTION

his book is about you. Stories are a part of who we are. As humans, we love creating and listening to stories. This love is part of us and always has been. And stories are incredibly powerful. They help us to make meaning from and understand the things that we feel and experience. Stories are a part of our identities, and we are a part of stories.

Some of our biggest and oldest stories are myths. Myths may try to explain things that seem like they cannot be explained, but there is more to myths. There is something that connects us to these stories underneath the tales of why and how: the feelings they express.

Mythological stories have been around for thousands of years because we connect with them and feel something when we read them. We relate to the characters and the trouble they get into. We might find that the imperfect god in the story is trying to make sense of a hard time, just like we are. Or we may see the mortals in these stories who are struggling to fit into the world, and that makes us feel seen. These stories show us something about who we are and who we want to be.

And in all these myths, there is—and has always been—queerness. None of the stories retold here have been significantly changed. They are being told now, in this moment, through my voice. But every single myth included in this book—plus many others, enough for whole other volumes— has a queer identity in it. Characters in countless myths are gay, lesbian, bisexual, pansexual, asexual, transgender, intersex, gender nonconforming, two-spirit, non-binary, and other LGBTQIA+ identities.

These identities reflect us, and they also reflect the people during the times the stories were first told. Queer people were part of every community. Some of the older myths are more than five thousand years old, and queer people are a part of them, even if labels, language, or definitions may have changed over time. What has always been true is proven true again by these stories: *we have always existed*.

In these twenty stories, I have kept the central parts of the myths— the "facts" about the fictional tales, if you will—true to the originals. Each myth has had many retellings over time. Sometimes each retelling adds or changes pieces, so I combined those with as many of the original parts as are known.

Sometimes when classic myths and stories are retold, identities are erased. For many myths, when some culture or group of people got a hold of the story, they began to remove aspects or reshape elements, or they tried to erase the story entirely. Even in modern myths and stories, there are people who are rendered invisible. But just as queer people have survived throughout time, these stories have persisted. Some of these myths have not been widely known for thousands of years. Others are myths that you may think you know but have more to learn about, particularly in the way queerness is a part of the story.

I chose to retell these stories you hold in your hands because of my own relationship to stories. I love stories; each and every day stories take up space in my mind and heart. I have always treasured myths. Not just classical myths, but also modern myths and true historic tales that read as myths. I am (and have nearly always been) an avid reader of comics and watcher of cinema and television, constantly looking at how stories get told and how they affect me and others around me. As a queer person, I can trace throughout my entire life the connections I made to stories because I saw myself in them. These connections were not just around queer identities, but that always added power to stories that I already found important.

I have many hopes for you, readers. I hope that no matter who you are, you can relate to each story in some way. And I hope that you are inspired to go out and learn more about each of these myths, or the countless others there are. (Be careful, though; mythology has a lot of trauma and violence embedded in it!)

Most importantly, I hope that everyone goes out and shares the myths that matter to them—that reveal something about who they are. Perhaps these are stories that you create, or perhaps you find other ancient stories to cherish. Perhaps you like true tales of history and seek out ways people with less visible identities start to show up in the stories we thought we knew. Or maybe you just keep returning to these stories here, sharing them far and wide, out loud (like the oral traditions of yore) or in print with the book you have in your hand now!

TU'ER SHEN
PROTECTS THE RABBITS

The myth of the rabbit god, who protects and safeguards queer love (particularly that of gay men), originates in the 1600s, or earlier, in China. Worship of the rabbit deity was illegal starting in the 1700s, though the myth was revitalized more recently, with temples celebrating the deity.

Hu Tianbao was a young man who lived his whole life in the same village. With his hair as black as the night sky, a constant smile across his slender face, and a sparkle in his eyes, he'd go out every day to explore the world around him.

Everyone in his community—his family, his teachers, his friends, and his neighbors—knew Hu Tianbao for his most treasured pastime: he loved learning. He took in all the sights, sounds, and feelings around him. To him, these observations were more than just information—they were feelings that Hu Tianbao could use to learn something new.

Each day, Hu Tianbao strolled from the library to the park. He was always looking for something. Every single time, he was searching. He looked for new places and new people. Or sometimes he'd notice how the same old places and the same old people would change around him. Sometimes the light hit a house differently, or the wind made a tree a whole new shape.

And in the bright-green grass in the central park, Hu Tianbao always found his favorite thing. Inevitably, a pointed ear sticking up, with the other flopped over, would emerge from the tall grass. It was a rabbit.

Hu Tianbao watched as many bright-white rabbits hopped up and down the hill—small rabbits, large rabbits, rabbits of all sizes. Some kept to themselves, while others huddled together. Some were still, staring around or wiggling their noses as they munched on some tiny shreds of grass. Others were actively hopping from place to place, dotting the hill as they moved about. Hu Tianbao's curious mind flitted like these rabbits—moving from rabbit to rabbit, idea to idea, place to place, person to person.

"Why do you like watching the rabbits so much, Hu Tianbao?" his friends would ask.

"They are agile, they are cunning, and they are friendly," he answered.

"But why is it that they fascinate you with their agility and their cunning?" they'd reply.

"They keep themselves safe. These beautiful, kind creatures in their quick movements are almost always free from danger. And their crafty, clever ways keep them and their families—even the rabbits that are not their relatives—all protected."

One day, as Hu Tianbao left the library to head to the park, he noticed something different emerge in his view: a visitor making regular stops in the village. The visitor was an inspector wearing a drab dark-blue uniform and carrying around a plain black satchel for his papers. Each week he visited to examine different parts of the village, then report back to the emperor.

Hu Tianbao became fascinated with what the inspector was learning during his trips. "What could I learn from him about the village?" he wondered. So Hu Tianbao sought out the inspector on each of his visits. And just as he found the white rabbits bouncing up the hill, he began to see this man bouncing around the neighborhoods, albeit with smaller ears! And he began to see the inspector as beautiful. He began to care for him, from afar, and wonder more about him.

Hu Tianbao found the inspector intriguing and attractive. He needed to learn everything about him he could. Every time the inspector—with his mesmerizing dark eyes and sharp, square jaw—came to visit, Hu Tianbao felt more jitters.

The feeling—the "jitters"—was the flutter of love growing inside him. His attraction grew and grew. His stomach felt like the pitter-patter of rabbits' feet hopping all over. And Hu Tianbao loved the feeling.

One day, while Hu Tianbao was watching the bunnies flitting around the green hills they so loved, he lost track of the inspector. But this time, the inspector had noticed Hu Tianbao, and he approached him with a scowl.

"Who are you and why do you watch me so?" asked the inspector.

"You fascinate me," replied Hu Tianbao.

"Why?" the cold, stern man demanded.

"You love learning and investigating, as do I. I feel lucky to have met you, almost like I have a lucky rabbit's foot, which I would never have because rabbits need their feet! And when I see you, I get these feelings—" continued Hu Tianbao.

The inspector cut him off and went back to the central city, far, far away from Hu Tianbao's village. The next day Hu Tianbao was arrested. The inspector had alerted the city officials to this exchange. At this time, in this place, these feelings were not allowed to be shared. Hu Tianbao was sentenced to death for his feelings. Even Hu Tianbao could not understand why this was happening. This situation was fueled by the one thing beyond his learning: hate.

Hu Tianbao was tragically killed because of his feelings. As his spirit descended to the underworld, Hu Tianbao was sure his story was not over. He knew that his time learning, exploring, caring, and protecting *could not* be over.

The underworld was abuzz upon Hu Tianbao's arrival. The other spirits—the ones who had been there the longest—had gathered. This council of the underworld nicknamed Hu Tianbao "Rabbit" because they knew of his curiosity. They saw his agility and understood the pitter-patter of love he experienced.

"Rabbit," they said, "you think you do not belong here. Why is that?"

"It was for my love that my life was taken, and it is for love that I will continue to fight," said Hu Tianbao.

The other spirits were confused. People weren't supposed to arrive in the underworld wishing to live. The spirits also worried about an injustice; no one was supposed to die in this manner.

"We can fix this," said one.

"We have to repair this," said another.

"Rabbit has more to do."

"He can protect others."

Suddenly, far away from the village Hu Tianbao lived and died in, a young villager had a peculiar dream. The young villager, a teenager, had just begun to feel his own jitters when he was with a friend at school. In his dream, he saw a rabbit. The rabbit was a beautiful white creature, with a sparkle in his eyes, hopping along a green hill. It was Hu Tianbao, or Tu'er Shen, the rabbit god, as the spirits called him now.

"I will protect you," said Tu'er Shen in the young villager's dream. "I will protect your love. Live in the world as you are. Fall in love and feel love. I will protect your affections. Know that I am here for you."

Since that dream occurred, anyone who felt affection of a queer nature could call upon Tu'er Shen. As the rabbits used their speed, agility, and cunning to protect themselves and one another from danger, Tu'er Shen would protect those who felt a love that was not accepted in the world.

ATHENA GAINS WISDOM

Athena is one of the most written about and well-known ancient Greek mythological characters. As an oral tradition, her stories existed well before the eighth century BCE. But Athena is not well-known for her romantic relationships, a trait all too common in stories of strong, independent female characters, and so her queer loves are rarely part of her mythology.

Athena had a lot going for her as the goddess of—among other things—wisdom. But wisdom and emotion do not always work in sync, and Athena had yet to realize this. In fact, on more than one occasion Athena's feelings interfered with her ability to be the wisest of beings, mortal or goddess.

Many stories were told about Athena's birth. They varied, but common among them was that she was born fully grown, which is why she was known for her wisdom. She simply knew what she needed to know. Athena's wisdom was highly revered, and her sense of strategy also made her the goddess of war. However, never one for needless conflict, she always strategized to resolve wars and bring about peace and, most important of all, justice. It was a constant balance for her.

Tragically—and perhaps ironically—the wisdom she used to guide so many others was not something she could readily apply to herself. Being wise and having life experience are two different things, and perhaps the lack of the challenges every other growing person goes through led her to make mistakes.

Athena fell in love with Myrmex, a maiden from Attica, who was also known throughout the land as one of the wisest mortals. Athena was always searching for someone who matched even a fraction of her own great wisdom. In this way, Myrmex was more than a match. Athena also found Myrmex physically beautiful, with a round figure and curly brown hair that framed her cherubic face. The two began a relationship, and Myrmex was deeply beloved by the goddess.

Athena also greatly admired Myrmex's passion for farming and her need to see everyone from her community properly fed. Myrmex's wisdom guided her toward such goodness, as she was always thinking about the ends before the means. But Myrmex wasn't all wisdom and altruism; she had a real trickster streak as well. Once Myrmex told some villagers that she was responsible for their good harvest, even though Athena knew this was not the case.

Athena and Myrmex wanted very much to help even more people get enough food, so they started to experiment with different ways of improving agricultural growth. Demeter, the goddess of the harvest, was responsible for the crops, but Athena wanted to go a step further to aid her love and their people. So Athena created the plow, sharing the important agricultural innovation with Myrmex so that all the crops could be harvested in greater quantities, ensuring everyone was fed well.

Shortly after, Myrmex took one of the plows and went to another village without Athena. There, she regaled the locals with stories of how *she* had invented the plow. She told them all the toil and trouble she went through and just how much of her wisdom and work went into this wonderful invention she bestowed upon them. They celebrated and honored Myrmex for her innovation, and she loved this feeling.

So Myrmex went to more and more places, telling more and more people about her invention and how it was only because of what she had done that they could even harvest their food. Word of "Myrmex's" invention spread far, soon making its way back to Athena.

Upon learning of Myrmex's lies, Athena was heartbroken. The very person Athena loved—and trusted—had betrayed her. It made the great goddess feel small, a feeling Athena hated so much that she decided Myrmex should feel small too. In a wave of anger, Athena turned Myrmex into an ant—in fact, the very first ant. Athena felt it was a fitting punishment. As an ant, a small insect that had to forage to survive, Myrmex was forced to eternally steal crops from others. And carrying a zucchini is no easy feat when you are smaller than a blade of grass!

Athena's father, Zeus—normally not known for his kindness and generosity—was appalled at Athena's actions. While he wouldn't reverse what Athena had done, despite being frustrated with his stubborn child's impetuousness, he was inspired to act in another manner. Needing to make a new species of human soldier, Zeus turned the newly proliferating insects into his army. He called these new soldiers "Myrmidons" in honor of Myrmex, the first ant.

Myrmex was not the only love of Athena's who caused her to lose her rational sense. Another time, Athena met the nymph Chariclo in the woods. Chariclo was a mystical being that presided over the woods and streams, as were all nymphs. Athena was drawn in by Chariclo's beauty and her love of nature. Chariclo was committed to the land, the water, and the animals within—all of which Athena found admirable.

As Chariclo and Athena's relationship progressed, they spent more and more time together in the woods, especially around the streams. They enjoyed the sound of the trickling water, particularly as it splashed against the rocks. They also loved following the paths of the winding streams, discovering what zigzags the powerful waterways carved in the land.

One day they bathed together in a small pond near some caves. It was private and was intended to be out of sight, as Athena—in her wisdom—found boundaries like this important. Meanwhile, Chariclo's son, Tiresias, was out playing with the snakes in the woods, following the creatures and studying how they slithered across the mossy ground. He came upon Chariclo and Athena in the pond and was shocked and embarrassed to spot his mother and her partner unclothed. Athena was even more shocked, and before even stopping to see who it was, she immediately blinded him.

Chariclo was stunned. She gathered up her robe, ran over to her son, and comforted him. Chariclo demanded that Athena give him his vision back, but alas, Athena was unable to reverse the damage she had caused. Recalling the regret that she felt over Myrmex and not wanting Zeus to intervene again, Athena tried to show mercy another way.

Athena gifted Tiresias with the sight of prophecy, granting him clairvoyance so he became known as a seer—a mystical oracle—despite his blindness. Athena, goddess of wisdom, finally began to consider the impact of her actions—and, more importantly, she began to recognize that those actions had consequences that couldn't always be reversed. This lesson ultimately enabled her to grow even wiser.

FLORINDA'S PRAYER

The Chilean folktale of Florinda was not recorded until the twentieth century, though it was passed down through oral tradition for centuries. It is a mixture of Indigenous beliefs—likely deriving from the Mapuche people of what is now Chile, Argentina, and Patagonia—and Christian ones. Many retellings describe the charm in the story as a crucifix. Whatever beliefs inspired this myth, the message is clear: Florinda's queerness is affirmed by her god.

As a child, Florinda was dark-haired, dark-skinned, short in stature, large in loving-kindness, and well-known in the town for her religious faith, even at this young age. She grew up with only her father, and that was never easy. Time and again, stemming from the desperation of supporting his family, Florinda's father would make terrible choices. He was not kind, nor was he thoughtful or decent. Florinda was not sure he had ever loved her. Her only solace was in a charm she held and meditated with nightly. Her charm was her way of connecting with her god.

When she was an adult, after meditating and praying with her charm, Florinda knew it was time to leave home; she had never been able to find work, and her father had no money. The only way for her to come into her own would be to escape from her father and this life. Florinda planned to use her father's horse to escape. Gathering her charm, the only thing that she cared about, she headed out. But Florinda knew that her father would come looking for her, so she disguised herself as a man using some of his clothes.

Florinda rode north for three days, guided by her faith and determination to find a better life for herself. She had scraped together what little food was left from her father's kitchen, but the meager morsels were not enough. She was nearly starved when she came upon a village. The local inn welcomed her, even though she let them know that she had no money. The innkeeper, a kind older woman, told Florinda that the village was known for its charity, and she simply had to request the king's approval.

A short time later, the king arrived and immediately approved the innkeeper's request to grant Florinda with food and a place to stay.

"Thank you for your kindness, Your Majesty," said Florinda. "I've been on the move for a few days and could not take care of my needs. My resources are slim, as I just left a horrible place behind me. All I have to give to others is my heart and my faith."

"Say no more, young man," said the king, fooled by her disguise and convinced she was a beautiful, kind young man from another village. "In fact, would you do me the kindness of staying a few more days? It would really help me."

Florinda agreed, uncertain why she was being asked to remain in town when she was the one in need of help.

Florinda did not realize that the king was planning to introduce her to his daughter, the princess. For months now, the princess had wanted to fall in love with and marry a kind man. The king decided, in his observation, that Florinda, with all his beauty, his faith, and his loving kindness, would be the best man for his daughter.

Over the next few days, Florinda and the king got to know each other and formed a bond. Florinda appreciated a father figure she could respect and even trust, someone unlike her own father in almost every way. The king appreciated the kind young man in front of him and the way that Florinda always led with his heart and spoke openly of his faith.

Finally, the king made his intentions known and told Florinda about his daughter. While the king had been kind to and supportive of Florinda thus far—and that kindness would continue—he was not offering a choice in the matter of his daughter. The king demanded that Florinda and his daughter be married the very next day.

That night, Florinda and the princess met for the first time. They had a magical dinner followed by a night out dancing. The chemistry between them was electric. When they got back to the inn and were alone, Florinda decided she had to be honest with the princess.

"Princess," said Florinda, in the gentlest, most truthful voice she could muster. "I am not a man. I have been in disguise because of some terrible trauma behind me. I didn't mean to trick you or anyone else in this town—all of whom have been so generous to me—but I need you to know I am not a man and I am not sure we can get married."

"Florinda," the princess said immediately, without a single pause. "I know that. I've known that since we met. I know we can be together. While a wedding tomorrow might be sooner than either of us would have normally agreed to, we can live together as two doves sharing a branch in a tree and find out if we are meant to be together forever."

Florinda's heart swooned, like a dove cuddling up to its partner, cooing and fluttering in the warm glow of its love and companionship.

The next day, the wedding proceeded, with Florinda still in her disguise. The king and queen thought Florinda was the most beautiful man they had ever known and that the couple were an incredible match, both in how they looked together and in who they were as people. They loved the couple so much that they decided to send a message to the princess's godparents to come and meet the happy couple.

The princess's godparents lived near the village, in a secluded area where fortune tellers, magicians, and witches all gathered. They consulted their friends the seers and found one fortune teller who claimed he could see not only secrets of the present, but also what was yet to come, which is, of course, something every good fortune teller should be able to do!

"Is the princess happy now that she is married?" the princess's godfather asked the capable fortune teller.

"Oh yes," the fortune teller replied. "She is extremely happy. She feels love, and she feels hope for the future. I can see all of that plain as those hideous shoes you are wearing, my liege!"

As the godfather adjusted his robes to hide his footwear, trying to ignore the criticism, he breathed a sigh of relief. "Well, it's settled, then."

"But wait," cried the fortune teller. "That is not all I see."

"Tell us," demanded the godmother, worried it might be more than just her husband's fashion sense. "Tell us so we can help our goddaughter avoid anything that robs her of that happiness."

"Well, she has married a woman," said the fortune teller.

Stunned, the princess's godparents had no reply. Their shocked looks conveyed their disbelief.

"Her husband is not a man, I can assure you of that," the fortune teller continued.

A short time later, the godparents arrived at the castle, doubting what they had heard, though not completely sure what to believe. When they met Florinda, they too were struck by her beauty, empathy, kindness, and compassion. But the words of the fortune teller were stuck in their minds. Not only had they changed their shoes, but they began to study Florinda in small ways. They observed what she wore, how she looked, and how she acted, trying to use this to confirm who she was. Using a narrow, out-of-date sense of gender kept them blinded by their own ignorance.

One day, the godparents decided to put Florinda to the test. They thought that no one but a man could capture a fox. The godparents and Florinda went into the woods to hunt one morning, and the godparents abandoned Florinda to see what would happen. Later that day, she returned with three foxes. Though Florinda let the foxes go, the godparents still felt sure she could not be a woman, and they questioned if what the fortune teller had said was true.

The princess's godparents decided to share the fortune teller's words with the king and queen. The king and queen couldn't believe that Florinda would ever deceive them like this, but the godparents could not quite let go of the fortune teller's words. The four elders devised one final test. They'd all go bathing in the river, where they could examine her body under her clothes, foolishly thinking that a body determined an identity.

The night before that trip to the river, Florinda was incredibly nervous, but the princess reassured her that they'd stay together no matter what.

At the river, Florinda arrived early to avoid being seen entering the water. The king and the godfather arrived soon after, and they all had a wonderful day under the hot sun in the cool water, splashing about, looking at the fish as they swam by, and retrieving some of the smoothed-over rocks at the river's bottom to keep as souvenirs of this special day together.

"Come on out, husband of my daughter; it is getting late and we must go," said the king.

"Yes, hurry out, fetch your clothes up on the shore, and let's go," said the godfather, conniving to get Florinda to expose her body.

As Florinda debated what to do, she thought she saw the charm she had prayed to for so long. It first appeared to be a reflection on the water's surface, and she was sure she was mistaken. But it began floating toward her in the air, as clear as day, and as it approached, the river rose in mist. Some say this mist masked Florinda's body so that her deception was not uncovered, while others speak of her body transforming. Whatever happened that day, Florinda's god had intervened on her behalf.

The king and the godparents never questioned Florinda again. They saw him for who he was, and Florinda knew that his god did too. Florinda lived his life as the princess's husband, and the two loving doves remained as happy as could be.

LONO AND KAPA'IHI
CONFRONT PRIDE AND PAIN

This combination of stories is part of Hawaiian religious mythology, an amalgam of Pacific Islander traditions. The story of Lono dates back to 500 CE, and his queer love story—of how finding a steadfast partner and living your truth can calm an otherwise vengeful god—continues to inspire love, peace, and forgiveness across the ages.

*I*magine, as a god, descending to Earth on a rainbow to live as a mortal man. This rather bombastic way to enter into the world was just how Lono-i-ka-makahiki—known as Lono—the king of Hawaii and god of creation, rain, and agriculture, arrived. It might have also been part of why he had a hard time seeing the negative effect he could have on people.

Lono led the people, including the armies of his lands, for a long time—too long to remember. He was known as the king, or chief, of Kona, also called the Big Island, and on every expedition, Lono looked all around him and saw the waves of committed soldiers, generals, and villagers.

Lono's fame went to his head, and he became difficult, even abusive. He was unkind to his soldiers and those who served him. He was so difficult that his wife left him. Lono was aggressive and dominating, and like the thunderstorms that were part of his domain, he was unpredictable and could even be catastrophic.

On one expedition, Lono's followers began to desert him. The exodus came with the fury of a storm. As Lono headed toward Kauai for his next

quest, he looked around and saw there was no one left. Lono had no idea why they had suddenly deserted him; all he knew was that he was left alone.

Lono persisted on his path to Kauai alone. On his journey, he noticed someone following him. The sneak was staying a safe distance back, but it was glaringly obvious that they were following Lono every step of the way. Lono waited on his boat along the beach to see who this follower was. If it was a straggling soldier from the army who perhaps decided not to join the rest in the rebellion, he did not want to scare them away.

The stranger got closer and Lono noticed his radiant smile, his shining eyes reflecting the ocean around them, and his dark, smooth-shaven head.

"Who are you?" Lono asked.

"I am Kapa-ihi-a-hilina. Most call me Kapa'ihi."

"But what are you doing following me?" asked Lono.

"It may seem odd. And while some of it might be from pity because everyone else has left you, it is more than that for me. There is something greater that brings me here to you, compelling me to follow you on this path," said Kapa'ihi, keeping his thoughts and feelings guarded, at least for the moment.

"I order you to tell me what it is that has you here with me," commanded Lono, who was starting to revert to the aggressive commander who had pushed everyone away.

"Stop that now," said Kapa'ihi, slowly, calmly, and patiently. His warm voice, deep and smooth, was soothing to Lono. "Do not speak to me that way, and do not choose anger or force over patience and warmth. You confuse your fires of passion, which come from the flame of creation, for the uncontrollable lava of rage and anger. I will not respond to you when you do that."

Lono was taken aback by Kapaʻihi's willingness to stand firmly but calmly. No one had ever pointed out to Lono that how he treated people was wrong. No one. Whether it was because he was a god or because he was their leader, he had never been confronted with a mirror. He paused to reflect.

For the first time, Lono apologized. "I am sorry, Kapaʻihi. I do not know you. You have been kind, and you made all this effort to be here with me, so I am sorry."

Kapaʻihi drew himself closer to Lono and continued. "Well, I would like to offer you companionship. I cannot explain it myself. I have been a part of the lands you ruled over for so long, and always I watched you and listened to you. I do not know how it happened, but I started to love you. So I followed you."

Lono was startled. No one, including his ex-wife, ever expressed anything like love to him, but he also never considered wanting it. Everyone around him always chose fear in response to him. Here was someone offering an alternative. Lono agreed that Kapaʻihi could join his quest.

In Kauai, Lono and Kapaʻihi searched for the rootless koa tree, a source of magical powers, of which Lono learned from communing with his spirit ancestors. But to find the tree and access its mythical potential, Lono was forbidden from using his own magical abilities. If he did, the koa tree would become an ordinary tree. The quest was tiresome and long, as Lono and Kapaʻihi moved over mountains and down beaches, through jungles and forests. The journey was made bearable only by their companionship. With little but leaves for clothing and bananas for food—and there are only so many ways to cook bananas—they struggled but persevered.

Ultimately Lono and Kapaʻihi found the koa tree, but that was not all. They also found that they were aikane, same-gender people who shared a deep type of love. Lono felt lucky to be finally experiencing this queer love after having heard of it for so long. Kapa'ihi had brought out the best in Lono. He listened to him and reassured him. When Lono chose anger or rage, or even just began to be commanding, Kapa'ihi would retreat, but never far. He'd always return with loving grace and offer Lono a reflection from which to grow and learn. Lono became more powerful and learned more magic through their aikane relationship than any tree or godly powers could have granted him.

Back on Kona, Lono gave Kapa'ihi everything and anything he could. The two never left each other's side, day or night. It was the happiest both had ever been. But then people started talking. Not everyone accepted aikane, and many did not want to see Lono happy after all the pain he had inflicted on others. When the gossip started to reach the couple, Kapa'ihi encouraged Lono to disregard it.

One day, Lono made Kapa'ihi a premier in the land, hoping that his loving-kindness, his grace, and—above all else—his patient listening could help more people. However, other officers and officials became jealous and angry. They did not trust Lono, with good reason, and they remained unwilling to accept Kapa'ihi.

The dissent reminded Lono of when everyone turned their backs on him. He could not face that again, and he refused to run the risk that he'd again be questioned and betrayed. He decided to leave the island. Lono's fear and mistrust made him turn his back on the one thing that brought him love and goodness. Since Lono refused to see Kapa'ihi anymore, Kapa'ihi was left in sadness. He felt the closest he ever had to anger, which was part resentment and part fear, unsure how to deal with Lono shutting him out.

After only a few days, Lono began to feel quite ill. He realized the choices he had made had destroyed all that he prized and that his emotional isolation was manifesting physically. Lono accepted that he could no longer choose rage, anger, and pride, and he went after Kapaʻihi.

Lono found his lover still crying on a nearby island. For days, Kapaʻihi had tried to deal with the breakup but was unable to; their love—their aikane—had been so great. Lono himself began to cry, in part from the pain he had caused his love and in part from the joy of being reunited. The rain now pouring from the heavens mirrored the tears streaming down his face. The pair's tears combined to form beautiful cascading streams in the land. With Kapaʻihi's forgiveness, he and Lono reunited happily, lovingly, and stronger than ever before.

ACHILLES AND PATROCLUS DISCOVER STRENGTH

The story of Achilles is central in Greek mythology, dating to perhaps the eighth century BCE. While it has been told and retold, scholars continue to debate Achilles's love of Patroclus in an ongoing erasure of his queer identity. This "debate" renders the partner he wished to spend the eternal afterlife with to a disputed footnote; instead their relationship should be fully reclaimed as an example of epic queer love.

Like most kids, Achilles didn't believe he had any weaknesses, but in his case, it might have been true! Achilles was known for having almost no vulnerabilities. When Achilles was just a newborn, his mother, Thetis, told him, "Achilles, you must be strong. Nothing must make you weak. If I could make you invulnerable, I would, because I want nothing to hurt you and for you to always be safe." She continued to repeat this every night even though he was a baby and could not understand her. (He was special, but not that special!)

As luck—or fate, or the gods—would have it, his mother found a way to do almost exactly as she wished. Thetis had tormented herself since Achilles was born with the fear that something terrible might happen to him. She did not know what, but like most mothers, she knew she could not imagine her beautiful, precious child being hurt in any way. With the help of her more resourceful and religious friends, she learned of a special ritual in the river Styx. When Achilles was just a small baby, she held him by his heels, dipped him in the waters of the river, and hoped it would make him invulnerable.

As Achilles grew, stories started to follow him that he was the toughest, strongest person alive. The stories also claimed his only weakness was the back of his heel, where his mother had held him, though Achilles never wanted to put these stories to the test.

Achilles was never one to stay still for very long. Whether it was a friend, a hobby, a favorite place, or even a book, he flitted about from thing to thing, place to place, person to person. He found that the longer he stayed someplace, the more at risk he was of discovering vulnerability or hurt. Keeping himself safe also kept him from a whole range of feelings.

Though he was nearly invulnerable, Achilles realized as he entered adulthood that something was missing. He had never found something or someone who excited him or around whom he could take risks.

Achilles did not have any siblings. Growing up with his mother and her friends made him inclined to be around people older than he. In school, it was always the older students to whom he gravitated, and once out of school he again found that his acquaintances—as he never really felt connected enough to call anyone a friend—were always a few years older.

One of those acquaintances was a leader in the local army, Patroclus. Achilles had known Patroclus for many years and even took on some work helping him. Patroclus was one of the kindest people Achilles had known, and he was always able to give Achilles the best advice. The admiration between the pair was mutual; Achilles seemed so wise to Patroclus. They each began to feel a reliance on the other.

When the hardened Achilles, who for so long had been protected from harm at the cost of his emotions, was around Patroclus, he was gentler. The people who knew them both started to take note and say things like, "Achilles, how do you feel about Patroclus?" to which Achilles automatically responded as he had his entire life, "I feel good. Things are fine." That protective armor that his mother had instilled in him had bound his heart in a calcified container.

But as the two became closer, Achilles started to name feelings that he had never been willing to name before. In the past, naming any feeling felt like a weakness, like his heel. But now he realized that he could find strength in the act of creating something new and in taking risks, for each risk was a lesson. He also realized that he could find strength in his love for Patroclus.

While their bond deepened and solidified, the rest of the world felt as though it started to loosen from its foundation. Battles became wars, and violence arose in more places than Achilles and Patroclus ever expected. They found solace in each other, and both remained committed to Patroclus's dedication to the army.

With the stories surrounding Achilles's supposed invulnerability widespread for so long, the enemies they fought demanded to see the hero in action. They taunted and begged for Achilles to join the battle.

Achilles wouldn't admit it to anyone except Patroclus, but he was scared. He was frightened that a lifetime of being told how strong, how near perfect he was, might mean that he was not ready. He was not prepared to be challenged or to be unsure, and that terrified him.

Patroclus decided to fight for his love, and without telling him, he donned Achilles's armor to fool the enemy, the warrior-prince Hector. Achilles learned of the ruse too late and went to find Patroclus, only to discover his love gravely injured. Patroclus begged Achilles with his dying breaths to allow himself to be vulnerable and to see the strength he had when he was. He wanted to see Achilles move on without him, assuring his love that one day they'd be reunited in the afterlife.

The man who never felt pain now experienced the deepest pain of all—grief and loss. Achilles called out to the gods, who told him that to avenge his love's death would be the end of his own life. But he did not care. He had no constructive ways to deal with the pain. Achilles murdered Hector, only to discover it did not make the grief go away. In fact, when Achilles saw Hector's wife—now a widow—herself stricken with grief, he realized that all he'd done was spread his own pain around. Somehow, she forgave Achilles for his act of murderous vengeance, an act of mercy that simply made him feel worse.

Achilles finally realized his invulnerability was not his strength, and as the gods had warned, by turning to revenge, he would lose his own life. Hector's brother, Prince Paris of Troy, took his revenge and fired an arrow right at Achilles's heel, murdering him.

Achilles had made one request just before his death: that his and Patroclus's bones be mixed in a vase when they were laid to eternal rest, to guarantee that they would find each other again. His request also made sure that everyone across time would know that Achilles's heel—his weakness—was not purely physical. Achilles's heel was the belief that being strong meant you could avoid vulnerability and pain. In fact, the opposite was true—one became strong only by allowing oneself to be vulnerable.

GHEDE NIBO
TELLS UNTOLD STORIES

This tale derives from Haitian and New Orleans–based myths relating to voodoo. Originating around the sixteenth century, these stories are part of the African diasporic religion. Ghede Nibo is still worshiped by practitioners today, and his power derives from his queerness, while his popularity probably also comes from his exquisite and extravagant appearance.

Ghede Nibo was a charismatic young man who loved investing his time and energy in his appearance. Like a peacock, he'd show off his plumage, typically in some variation of black and purple clothing, along with his trademark top hat and cane. The garments often sparkled and shimmered and were made from some of the finest fabrics and patterns that could be found.

Ghede Nibo identified his gender as he but often performed drag onstage at balls as she. Ghede Nibo, like the peacock, loved to display his beauty through many genders, and his appearance was another way in which he got to creatively express himself. Ghede Nibo always dedicated his performances to Baron Samedi and Marman Brigitte, the infamously over-the-top spirits that ruled over the realm of the dead. Baron Samedi was known for his all-black ensembles, long coattails, and dark glasses, always with splashes of white accessories and makeup, giving the illusion that he was wearing his skeleton outside his skin. Marman Brigitte was known for her plumes of black rooster feathers and the sparkles all over her body, as she busily guarded the grave sites of the recently passed, shifting in and out of the darkness. Ghede Nibo took inspiration from both.

Tragically, while still young, Ghede Nibo was murdered. Fortunately, death was not the end for him. Baron Kriminel, a powerful and shady Iwa—or voodoo spirit—was notorious for possessing people to do horrible things. It was one of those poor souls that the baron possessed who took Ghede Nibo's life. When Ghede Nibo arrived in the realm of the dead, the spirits had no idea what to do with such a remarkable tragedy, which—legend had it—was the first murder ever committed.

Baron Samedi and Marman Brigitte decided they could add one more member to their house, so they adopted Ghede Nibo, for they had never met someone whose life had been taken by another. The pair, known always for their eccentric traits and quirks, made Ghede Nibo feel right at home. Baron Samedi was also the spirit in charge of resurrection. Together with Marman Brigitte, he decided that there was more good to come from Ghede Nibo being a spirit deity than would come from resurrecting him to a mortal life, and the two transformed him.

Now a powerful spirit, Ghede Nibo leaned into the things that set him apart as a mortal man, so he himself became even more extroverted and extravagant. Ghede Nibo regularly performed in drag on the runways in the realm of the dead. And in the realm of the living, he'd frequently inhabit mortal bodies, compelling them to perform in their own drag and play with their expressions of themselves in all sorts of colorful ways. His acts brought Ghede Nibo—and those he possessed—bliss. This bliss was healing, as were the medicinal herbs that Ghede Nibo always carried, ready to place them in the realm of the living where they could most come to someone's aid.

Anointed Prince of the Cemetery, Ghede Nibo soon discovered that living a life—and an afterlife—as a drag queen gave him special abilities the other spirits did not have. He could speak to different types of spirits and could commune with the spirits of any realm. He could also speak on behalf of the spirits, passing on messages to the realm of the living. He found a special place in between living and dead—known as a liminal place—that was uniquely his in which to travel.

Ghede Nibo had always had a fondness for animals, and the spirits he was able to commune with included those of animals. Once he came upon several horses in the realm of the dead. The horses, known as his chevals, became his dear friends and helped to ferry him from realm to realm, spirit to spirit, even faster than before.

As Ghede Nibo and his chevals listened to the voices of the dead, transmitting messages to and from the realm of the living, they began to hear other voices, like faint whispers underwater, calling to them below the regular spirits. Ghede Nibo and his chevals sought these whispers out, only to discover they were spirits trapped and wandering aimlessly.

These were the spirits of people who had died suddenly in an accident or from an illness or other tragedy, and so when their spirits reached the realm of the dead, they did not know what had happened and became adrift. They were left wandering in that space, as if they were trapped underwater, where they could not be heard by any other spirits. Ghede Nibo was determined to assist them to sashay to their rightful homes, but he would need someone in the realm of the living who could help discover what had happened.

"Please, help, we cannot understand what has happened to us; we lost our eleganza," the wandering spirits pleaded.

"Can you help us get a message through to our loved ones?" others asked.

Sometimes their questions were as simple as "What did I do to deserve this shade?" or "Can you give me life?" and Ghede Nibo would return to them with as many answers as he could to help them settle down in the afterlife. He took these specters under his care, becoming known as a guardian of all spirits who died too soon.

Enlisting the help of Ghede Masaka, a trans spirit whose power allowed him to manifest easily in the mortal realm, Ghede Nibo and his chevals could commune with not just the spirits, but also the people who visited grave sites. Being able to take form in the realm of the living meant Ghede Masaka could also unearth the graves of those trapped to discover the stories the spirits needed to share. Sometimes, if the remains were lost, Ghede Nibo and his chevals, with Ghede Masaka's help, set out to find the bones or some other personal trophy that was close to the person who passed, so that their trapped soul could be laid to rest.

Ghede Nibo and Ghede Masaka also helped find the spirits' loved ones and the people they cared about in their communities. They shared the stories of what had happened, and they assured those still living that the spirits had moved on, bringing them resolution by telling their stories. Ghede Nibo was uniquely positioned to give these spirits a voice, having inhabited and traveled the in-between space—even when he was alive—which now enabled him to make sure every voice was heard and every story was told.

Ghede Nibo served as the patron and guardian of one more group of spirits, perhaps the most important to him: he became the caretaker of the souls of children who died. Regardless of their age or cause of death, to Ghede Nibo, all children who died were passing on before their time and needed his help. Ghede Nibo loved being with these spirits the most. He sang them songs and told them stories. He performed for them, finding all the different ways he could be in drag. Through his storytelling and drag, he was able to communicate something all children wanted: affirmation. Ghede Nibo helped all spirits find peace, acceptance, and most of all love.

MAWU-LISA
CREATES EVERYTHING

This universe creation story is part of the mythology of the Dahomean religion, which originates in the beliefs and traditions of the Fon people in Benin, Africa. This myth was part of their culture in the 1600s, though it likely predates that period as an oral tradition among local tribes. This narrative connects how the world came into being to the way queerness—fluidity— is woven into all things.

Mawu, goddess of the moon and creator of souls, and Lisa, god of the sun and creator of tools, were so old that they existed even before creation. The two gods seemed in some ways to be in perfect balance, proof that not every pair needed to be opposed.

Mawu was an older female deity. At her heart, she was a creator. Mawu was the one who created people, initially with clay. When the clay material eventually started to run out, she began to reuse other bodies and beings. This is why people sometimes feel like they recognize someone they have never met before.

Mawu was also known for the night. It was with the darkness of the night that she was able to provide people with the ability to navigate the unknown. Mawu hoped that by becoming comfortable with the dark, people would express more gentleness and forgiveness—two qualities that help people embrace the uncertain. The act of creation brought her much joy, and that joy was infectious, constantly being transfused to all in the world.

Lisa, on the other hand, was a much younger male deity. He was also known as a god who liked to be in the light. Whether it be by the warm rays of the sun or the bright beaming light of fire, Lisa loved to work all day, and working helped him develop strength. While Mawu worked persistently at creation, Lisa was furiously building functions, systems, and structures.

The universe was filled with an immense amount of chaotic and intense energy, a small fraction of which Mawu and Lisa used for their purposes. One time, this energy of the universe exploded with its fierceness. As a result of this explosion, Mawu and Lisa were fused together to become the ultimate god: Mawu-Lisa.

As Mawu-Lisa, they were now a single being, made up of every part of both their male and female halves. Mawu-Lisa was non-binary while also encompassing the entire spectrum of gender identity. Mawu-Lisa was also now the most powerful among the deities.

Over four days, Mawu-Lisa shaped, ordered, and added to everything they had already made. Everything in the universe worked because of their union. They were also a paradox—a contradiction—because they represented so many different energies. These paradoxes showed up all over creation, which worried Mawu-Lisa.

Mawu-Lisa grew concerned that their creation was imbalanced. They knew the importance of balance and realized that despite their combined strengths, they needed help. So they reached out to their fellow deity Aido-Hwedo, a serpent.

Aido-Hwedo coiled themself around the world, supporting it and everyone in it in case of accidents or shifts. The coils wrapped around everything Mawu-Lisa created, and by wrapping themself around it, Aido-Hwedo provided the universe with stability.

Aido-Hwedo, now also known as Da the World Serpent, was always there to support and provide structure. Anytime someone in the universe sees a rainbow, there is Aido-Hwedo. Whenever that shimmering array of colors appears, whether in the sky, or in a reflection on water, or through a prism, it is the energy of the supremely supportive love that Aido-Hwedo bestowed upon Mawu-Lisa's world.

The well-being of all the universe remained supported by the structure of Aido-Hwedo, by the fluidity of Mawu-Lisa, and above all else by love. Mawu-Lisa and Aido-Hwedo's commitment to all beings was in fact exactly what a world filled with change, complexity, and contradiction needed to shine and thrive.

ANANDA'S SELFLESS LOVE

The stories of Ananda were first told during the fourth or fifth century BCE in India. Though they are written like many myths as a true accounting of someone's life, it is unclear who the real Ananda was. This particular myth of Ananda and Cobra navigating healthy limits in love comes from the Theravada school of Buddhism and is one of the Jataka tales—ancient origin fables from India dating back to shortly after the time of Buddha's life.

Ananda's fate was practically predetermined at birth, with his name meaning "joy and bliss." Ananda found he was happiest when he could give love. He'd loved his family since he was a baby. When he became a teenager, Ananda's first boyfriend was Sriputra. Ananda thought about Sriputra every day and felt like the love he had to give him was infinite. But when Sriputra died tragically, Ananda became deathly ill. He trembled endlessly and felt like a poison had taken over his body, though it was only his heartbreak. Luckily, his twin brother, Pandu, was there to comfort and support him, and he recovered soon after.

A few years later, still young men, Ananda and Pandu lost their parents. The loss was hard on them; their parents had been their comfort and protection. Ananda and Pandu became hermits as a result, shutting themselves away from the world to rebuild their lives. Grief and loss did not become easier for Ananda.

But Ananda, as always, had a lot of love to give. One day at the river, he met another young man, whom he found beautiful. Everything about this slender man sparkled—his dark hair, his eyes, his smile. Every day they'd talk and talk and talk at the river. Finally, Ananda started to feel love again. Ananda and the man, who he learned later was called Cobra, fell in love.

Ananda and Cobra could not live without each other. But Cobra had a secret: he was not even human. Living up to his name, Cobra was, in fact, a shape-shifting jewel-neck cobra. And when Cobra revealed his true form, Ananda was even more fascinated by him. They'd spend time talking to each other as Cobra coiled around Ananda to comfort him.

Whenever Cobra left, Ananda grew sick. Ananda was afraid of getting as ill as he had when he lost Sriputra, so he asked his brother for help.

"Do you still want Cobra to visit you each day?" asked Pandu.

"I do," replied Ananda. "But I do not like feeling the loss I feel when he leaves. I find the feeling overwhelming, and I have no control."

"Since Cobra is a jewel-neck cobra, you can pretend that all you care about is his prized neck jewel. If he thinks all you value is material wealth, he will reject you," plotted Pandu.

Ananda agreed. Though he did not like to lie, he needed a plan to help free him from this overwhelming feeling of love that bordered on obsession. The next day, when Ananda saw Cobra, he told him he wanted the jewel and that was why he was spending time with him.

"I do not know if that is true, Ananda," said Cobra. "I have felt what you have felt, and I know we felt it together. But if it is true, I have been sadly mistaken. And if it is not true, you are lying to me. So either way, I will take leave of you."

Cobra left, and Ananda started to feel ill. He returned home to his brother, who had to take care of him for a few days while he recovered. Ananda's illness was even worse than it had been when he lost Sriputra. But time softens most pain, and even if it does not heal, it scabs over.

Ananda eventually recovered himself enough to live his life and never saw Cobra again.

Over the course of his life, Ananda channeled his love into other projects. He advocated for nuns—the women in his religious practice—to be able to make decisions for themselves. He fought against restrictive gender norms, remembering—as did the other devotees of his religion—his own past lives as male, female, and non-binary genders. He turned his spiritual practice into a vocation and became a monk, building community among his fellow monks and forming sewing circles so that they could all engage in the act of creation together.

Ananda loved all humans, and his circle of compassion was wide. But his closest friend—truly, the love of his life—was the Buddha. Ananda was completely devoted to the Buddha, and the two grew close over a long friendship. Once when his dear Buddha became ill, Ananda became ill too, unable to separate his sympathetic feelings from his physical ones. He cared for Buddha and took care of him as a loving partner does.

But love was attachment, and for so long Ananda had been told to release his attachment by his love, Buddha, who was guiding his spiritual practice. His earthly attachments, including his deep love for Buddha, prevented his becoming immortal in the afterlife. Ananda never understood how love could be bad, but he also wasn't sure he completely understood what love was.

Ananda tried to learn how to balance attachment with safety. With each love he felt, he learned more about boundaries and self-love. For the rest of his life, Ananda remained devoted to Buddha but finally learned that giving love also required him to take care of himself. Ananda knew that in his next life, when reincarnated, he would finally be lightened of the weight of attachment and able to love freely and healthily, starting with himself.

HERMES'S GIFTS

The story of Hermes—also known as Mercury—is one of the more famous Greco-Roman myths, possibly originating in oral form as early as 2000 BCE (it first appeared in written form centuries later, around 800 BCE). While many Greco-Roman myths include violence and toxicity, what holds true across the myths of Hermes are the connections he makes and their importance in his life.

Perhaps most known around the world as a style connoisseur, with his winged sandals and matching helmet and staff, Hermes spent most of his time as the messenger for the countless communications of mortals and immortals, heroes and villains alike. As Hermes sat in Olympus, realizing he was in his twilight, he kept thinking about the connections he had made as the herald of the gods. Love is the primary connection across most people's lives, and Hermes was no exception when it came to the people who meant something to him throughout his years.

When Hermes was young, he had a reputation for being a trickster god, and his exploits were infamous. As just a baby, he targeted his brother Apollo with one of his pranks. Escaping from his crib—no small feat for a child; Hermes was anything but typical—he absconded with fifty of Apollo's most prized cows. Most babies are satisfied with milk; Hermes wanted the whole cow! He displayed the unsurpassed cleverness of his deception by leading the cows backward—covering all their tracks—to make sure no one knew where he took them. Not only that, but baby Hermes also fashioned fake hoofprints with a makeshift shoe that created a trail that led elsewhere. These shenanigans led to the first of many confrontations and trials for Hermes.

When he was a young man, Hermes tried the cow trick again. This time, the owner of the cattle was a farmer named Perseus. He was beautiful, kind, and merciful. Perseus discovered Hermes in the act of mischief but forgave him right away and invited him inside to explain why he had decided to steal the cows. This exchange blossomed into a relationship that Hermes cherished as one of his earliest loves. It was a love born not just from his trickster impulses, but from the mercy granted him.

The soon-to-be-notorious witch Circe, who had not yet met Odysseus, was another of Hermes's strongest connections. Hermes visited her island in between his many trips as messenger of the gods. The island was beautiful, with dense woodlands just in from the beaches and shores, and filled with various flora and fauna. At each turn, one could discover some creature's gentle call or a plant's colorful expression.

Hermes and Circe spent much time sharing stories with each other. With every visit Hermes made, each tried to one-up the other to determine who was the best storyteller. Slowly their time together evolved into something more, and the two began an intimate relationship. However, both knew this was not an enduring love. Circe wanted her freedom as she cultivated both her magic and her land. Hermes wanted his own independence, as he knew he could never settle down in any one place. So the two talked through their boundaries, establishing a relationship that worked for them. They enjoyed their exchange of stories for some years, never crossing a boundary in their relationship that would complicate their lives together.

Hermes also found love with Amphion, a son of Antiope, an Amazon and child of the god of war. When the two met, Amphion was lost and adrift, without much of a dream. In contrast, Hermes was feeling inspired at this point in his life and wanted to find a way to share that with Amphion. As Hermes and Amphion spent time together, Hermes learned that Amphion loved music. He gifted Amphion a lyre he made by placing string over a wooden stick; Amphion, however, had never been taught music. Hermes remedied that, teaching him to sing, play, and dance. Each time Hermes was on a journey, he'd find a new object with which to make another instrument and bring it back to Amphion so they could create beautiful music together. While their love did not endure the distance between them, they remained always connected through Amphion's poetry and song, celebrating the love they'd shared.

It was the call of travel that Hermes most often wanted to heed. Being a messenger was how he met one of his greatest, most enduring loves. For what seemed like years after they had met, Hermes and Aphrodite, goddess of love and beauty, would pass like sailing vessels in the night.

Zeus, king of the gods, saw a budding connection between Hermes and Aphrodite. Never one to shy away from intervening, Zeus had an eagle retrieve Aphrodite's sandal without her knowing and bring it to Hermes. As the messenger of the gods, Hermes was eager to get it back to her. They flirted a bit more than usual that day, and as they did so, a door opened to a relationship that grew over time. Hermes and Aphrodite eventually fell deeply in love and had a child. Their child, Hermaphroditus—whom they loved so deeply—was known for being non-binary, possessing not just aspects of the male and female genders, but male and female bodies as well.

The stories of Hermes and his many loves—more than just these few—were often about the gifts he gave them. He gave Aphrodite her sandal, Amphion his lyre, Perseus his own cows back, and Circe her stories. But as Hermes reflected on his life, it was not the gifts he gave to them that mattered. It was the gifts they gave to him in return—their love. Hermes always had their love to hold on to, and that was something he could take wherever he ran.

HI'IAKA AND WAHINE-OMAO SEEK SUPERHEROIC ADVENTURE

This epic and timeless superhero story is part of Hawaiian religion, made from an assortment of Indigenous and Polynesian cultures that have fused over millennia. Hi'iaka's story dates back to approximately 500 CE. It is the story both of a fierce superheroic warrior and of her queer love.

Hi'iaka was a superhero as well as a Kapua, a magical entity related closely to the gods. Even before she was born, her story was filled with adventure. Her sister Pele—the Kapua of volcanoes, fire, and creation—carried Hi'iaka around as an egg. Pele knew Hi'iaka was special and wanted to protect her, and the fires of Pele were enough to help incubate the egg until Hi'iaka was born. Her name, in fact, means "to carry an embryo."

Hi'iaka was the Kapua of hula dance and magic. She was also a Kapua of nature, with clouds and forests in her purview, as well as healing and all natural magic. Though she was tasked with overseeing all these things, she craved adventure most of all.

Everything Hi'iaka did became an adventure. For her, hula dance was an adventure with her body, telling stories and reciting poems that honored and celebrated her people's history. Natural magic was an adventure that brought together the land and the spirits. Healing was an adventure, making sure that forests could grow and the land was healthy, so that the people living on it were too.

Hi'iaka loved the forest, as it had great potential for adventure. Magic was stronger there, and forest bathing was healing for everyone. With the leaves of plants from the lush island forests, hula skirts were made by all the island residents as an honor to Kapuas, local leaders, and to the forest itself. Everything seemed to come from the forest. And, of course, adventure over land and through forests of dense trees filled with unknown mysteries inspired heroes across time. In one such forest, Hi'iaka met and fell in love with Hopoe. Hopoe was a mortal who had helped Hi'iaka develop hula and spread the tradition across the land. Despite this magical partnership, Hi'iaka and Hopoe's love did not last, and they soon ended their relationship. The two remained dear friends.

As Hi'iaka wandered from island to island, through the forests in which she felt strongest, she waited for her epic adventure. While she appreciated her many smaller adventures, Hi'iaka wanted a big one, an adventure that people would remember forever. She wanted stories to be written about her and not just her siblings. But Hi'iaka needed a quest.

Finally, just the quest arrived. Her sister Pele asked Hi'iaka to find Lohiau, an island chief she once loved and had not seen in a very long time, as Pele always struggled to let go of those she loved and felt a need to close the distance between them. Hi'iaka readily agreed but made two requests in return. First, Hi'iaka asked Pele to maintain her precious forests in her absence. Second, Pele had to keep Hi'iaka's dear friend Hopoe safe.

For her journey, Pele gifted Hi'iaka three things: the eye of foresight, allowing her to receive knowledge from the spirits and see pieces of possible futures; powerful arms and legs, which granted her the strength to protect herself and others; and a skirt made of lightning, which granted her enhanced magical powers, including control of the clouds. With these gifts, Hi'iaka became the ultimate superhero, no cape needed.

After saying goodbye to Hopoe, Hi'iaka began her epic quest, joined by Pau-o-Palai, a faithful friend to Pele and her whole family. With Pau-o-Palai at her side, Hi'iaka went on adventure after adventure, defeating evil creatures and saving countless lands, using her gifts to guide her. Storytellers from every land started to spread word of Hi'iaka's feats. But everyplace the duo went, they could not find Pele's lost love, Lohiau.

As they ventured through stunning, lush lands, they encountered many people. On one part of their journey, they came upon Wahine-Omao, a beautiful and pious woman, roughly Hi'iaka's age, shepherding her many pigs with her as she traveled to a ritual to honor Pele. Nicknamed "the Green Woman" because of her connections to the plants and the land, Wahine-Omao was actually a mortal—though anyone who shepherds a dozen pigs many miles has superhuman patience! She was also the most beautiful creature Hi'iaka had ever seen, with shiny black hair that sat high on her head, and bright, near-white eyes set in her dark-caramel skin. While Hi'iaka did not want to be distracted from her quest, she had to stop and learn more about Wahine-Omao.

Upon learning of Wahine-Omao's upcoming celebration to honor Pele, Hi'iaka exclaimed excitedly, "Pele is my sister! What are the chances that I would come upon someone so beautiful who was so committed to my family?"

"I always admired her spirit," said Wahine-Omao. "I believe she has guided me through much of my life, and now I am honored to come upon you, which I think her guidance is responsible for."

Hi'iaka was entranced by Wahine-Omao's beauty and her positive, creative energy. "Wahine-Omao, would you join our epic quest?" she asked.

"Yes," replied Wahine-Omao, "once I finish this ritual to honor the strength and power of the volcano and all of nature, as we will need that guiding force no matter where we go."

Hiʻiaka's eye of foresight tingled, and with that she knew Wahine-Omao's words were true. "Yes, I see now that the forest and the volcano will be of the utmost importance between us, Wahine-Omao. Let us proceed on your journey." Simply saying "us" when referring to her and Wahine-Omao made the rest of Hiʻiaka tingle. She awaited discovering how the forest and the volcano would become a part of their story.

After months together, Pau-o-Palai departed to seek her own adventures, leaving Hiʻiaka and Wahine-Omao to continue on their own. As they traveled, they began to fall in love. Word of their adventures continued to spread, and Hiʻiaka and Wahine-Omao became known throughout the lands as the ultimate heroes.

Together, the pair finally found Pele's lover, Lohiau, after which they decided to settle down for a time. They reveled in the stories told of their epic quest. They never rested for long; the pull of adventure continued to call. Sometimes it called Wahine-Omao, and she went off to brave the forest and protect the creatures that lived there. Sometimes adventure called to Hiʻiaka, and she headed out to use her three gifts, always to protect the land and sea.

The two were close, with a trust, love, and intimacy that Hiʻiaka had never imagined possible. Even when they were apart, Hiʻiaka never felt the loss over distance that Pele had once described. Both Hiʻiaka and Wahine-Omao knew and trusted that the other would be okay.

As they ventured apart and returned together—always together—Hiʻiaka discovered she could use her magic to reach Wahine-Omao when they were separated. Calling upon the magic within her, she could send her loving thoughts via the lava plains or forest trees. Each time the lovers were separated, Wahine-Omao simply needed to watch the beautiful, intense flow of lava or look up at the way the breeze moved the forest canopy above her head, and she felt Hi'iaka with her. Hi'iaka's earlier glimpse into the future had come true. The forest and the volcano became a part of their love. Their love was a part of the natural world around them—it transcended space and time. And with the security of their love in place, they were truly able to be superheroes to the world.

CORYDON SHEPHERDS HIS COMMUNITY

❧

The stories about the shepherd Corydon cross over the mythologies of the Greek and Roman cultures—as do many of their gods and goddesses. Originating in perhaps the 300s BCE, Corydon's story is brief, though the character has shown up in many tales, confirming that his willingness to love bravely and boldly has fascinated many over eons.

Growing up on a farm in Athens was not always easy for Corydon. He was a creative and excitable child, bouncing around from the nearby village to neighboring farms so often that the other villagers called him a ked—a tiny, wingless, reddish-brown bug that quickly moved from sheep to sheep on all the farms. Under the villagers' breath and behind the backs of Corydon and his family, the whispers had a worse meaning: keds were unwanted pests, sucking the blood from sheep, and Corydon was unwanted by most villagers. The neighbors wished Corydon could act like the other boys did and preferred that he stay away if he was going to be so different.

Corydon knew he was different and was aware that nearly everyone around him knew it too. His family was loving and generous and always allowed him to be himself—ked or no ked. They kept the rules at home flexible so that he could express himself. He was allowed to be creative and to dance, to move his body fluidly. Sometimes he wanted to dress in a unique way, with bright colors and fabrics that he found discarded by the local tailor.

Corydon simply wanted the space and freedom to be himself. But the wider community made it hard. Among the other farms and the townspeople, expectations were rigid, and the smallness of the town and his neighbors' minds—smaller, he felt, than the minds of the insects they referred to him as—made him wish he could escape.

But Corydon also loved being on the farm. He loved the fruits and flowers he grew with his family. And he loved the sheep most of all. One day, when he was still a young man, he met the beautiful Alexis, a fellow shepherd who loved his trade. Alexis was about Corydon's age, but unlike Corydon, who was tall and broad, Alexis was slender and nimble-looking. He had long hair that hung to his shoulders but somehow still looked weightless. His eyes caught Corydon's every time they passed each other in the fields, and Corydon's heart buzzed.

Corydon was in love with Alexis, and for a while it seemed that Alexis might have the same feelings. They would stop to see each other across a fence and talk about their days, or they'd take a stroll through the trees lining the field, looking for the latest bloom or some colorful berry to pick off a bush as the shepherd dogs tended the sheep. Whenever Alexis was away trading supplies in another village, Corydon missed him deeply.

Finally, Corydon decided it was time to act, time to let Alexis know how he felt. As a token of his affection, he gifted Alexis a few goats, berries and other fruits he foraged, and a wreath of flowers that he strung together so it could be worn as a necklace. Along with the gifts, Corydon shared that he hoped they could be more than friends. But Alexis revealed his heart was elsewhere—with a maiden in the trading village. Although his heart was promised to another, there was still room in it for the goat, so he accepted Corydon's gifts happily, though the two would drift apart.

Corydon was heartbroken but took solace in the fact that Alexis did not make fun of him. He did not express any offense or dismiss Corydon because of his feelings. He simply rejected him because there was someone else. Not everyone was that understanding, which scared Corydon. Even as a young man, he remained fearful that people would find out who he was and that those whispered insults would be spoken aloud.

Despite those fears, Corydon's first love wouldn't be his last, thanks in part to Pan, the god of music, the wild, and shepherds. Corydon was comforted by the stories of Pan and how Pan loved others regardless of their gender. Corydon often sat to meditate, with Pan in mind, by the streams and caves in the woods to find solace.

Taking up a small wooden flute he had carved, Corydon sought to embody Pan's peaceful nature in his everyday life. Now well into adulthood, Corydon played music as he strolled through the fields and the forests each day. He'd sing and play the flute, and his voice along with the melody of the instrument created a beautiful musical tribute to honor Pan. He hoped that all creatures who could hear him, human and otherwise, could find a moment of bliss in nature.

One day while Corydon was out playing his flute in the woods, he heard a song. The voice was unfamiliar but lovely, and he wanted to know to whom it belonged. He came upon a man just a few years older than him, but with silver-gray hair cut close to his head. The sun, shining through the tree-tops, reflected off his light hair, and his dark skin seemed to glow. Corydon was extremely attracted to the musician, who introduced himself as Thyrsis.

Corydon and Thyrsis shared stories with each other about their lives. Though Thyrsis was a shepherd like Corydon, he was mostly known for his singing. Time and again, he bested traveling singers and storytellers with the beautiful instrument that was his voice. He had plenty of practice singing to his quite willing audience of sheep! As day turned to night, Corydon asked Thyrsis to join him back at home, and he agreed.

The next day, in a teasing fashion, the two decided to compete to see who possessed the best singing voice. Thyrsis insisted they needed towns-people to judge, which made Corydon uncomfortable. After all, Thyrsis was a seasoned competitive singer. But Corydon reluctantly agreed, so the two went to the village. Everyone in the community began to assemble, includ-ing all those people who had judged Corydon since he was a child.

They both sang the stories of their lives—Thyrsis about his shepherd-ing travels, Corydon about love. The two were nearly matched in how beau-tifully they sang, and the town was enchanted. It was as if the god Pan had put everyone under his spell, and they relished the beautiful harmony, absorbing the tales of these two men. The songs connected the townspeople to one another and to the natural world around them. But, most of all, the songs connected them to Corydon and Thyrsis.

To his surprise, Corydon won the competition! The town had chosen him. Though it was Thyrsis's first loss, he was not upset, as he could see that Corydon had found his voice. And in experiencing Corydon's voice, the community finally realized the error of their ways: that they shouldn't have judged someone unique, beautiful, and different.

Thyrsis continued with his travels, while Corydon stayed behind. He forgave the townspeople and became a central part of the community. He sang them stories nearly every day—when the sheep were where they needed to be, of course! And they would come help him with the farm and ask him questions about his life. They wanted to know more about what happened with Alexis and just why Thyrsis was so special to him. They were curious and open, and because they were focused on being nonjudgmental, they found themselves instead filled with love.

One day while playing his flute in the woods, Corydon encountered a short, stocky, dark-haired man with mesmerizing silver eyes. This man, named Glaucon, was looking for work at a nearby farm. He lived in the mountains but came down to seek different pastures. He was a reverent of Pan and carried his own flute in his satchel. With few words exchanged between them, Corydon and Glaucon began playing together.

Their music appeared to last for days, even years, as together they fell under the spell of Corydon's beloved god, Pan. Their love felt as though it was blessed by the great god. The two remained together as a part of the caring community around them—a community that began to love truly only when they let go of preconceptions and became bravely open to loving boldly.

FET-FRUNERS'S
BLESSED CURSE

The story of Fet-Fruners originates in an Eastern European Romanian folktale that has existed in writing since at least the nineteenth century. Orally, the myth is much, much older, possibly five hundred years or more. It stands out for its remarkable affirmation of the main character's gender transition and euphoria as well as for its story of love and adventure.

here was once a kingdom ruled over by Emperor Coman, who made many demands of those around him. One day, he'd ask every village for their gold—whatever they had mined or traded. The next, he'd ask for potatoes, which were as priceless as gold but much tastier, and each village gathered up all they had—even from their own pantries or plates—and sent it to the empire's capital. Emperor Coman's demands were extreme and constant.

A local village's mayor, named Florian—who was also a magician—grew more and more tired of complying with the emperor's demands. The magic Mayor Florian had practiced since he was a boy was not enough to change anything, but he kept seeking a way to stop the emperor.

Mayor Florian had three children, known in the village as the princesses, each with her own spirit and commitment to the community. Neither of the older two princesses had spirit quite like the mayor's youngest, Fet-Fruners. Fet-Fruners had chosen their name when they came of age, and most of the village had long since forgotten the name with which they were born. Additionally, Fet-Fruners did not feel "princess" was the best way to describe them. Fet-Fruners's sisters seemed comfortable as princesses, as daughters, and as women. But Fet-Fruners did not share that comfort. Luckily their father and siblings allowed them to be themselves.

One day, Emperor Coman demanded that each village send forth a prince to join his royal army. In exchange, Emperor Coman would no longer demand any gold, potatoes, or other tax for ten years. Mayor Florian knew that for the benefit of his people, he had to comply. Ten years was a long time for his people to be able to enjoy their own gold—and ten years of potatoes made a lot of meals!

For Fet-Fruners's two older siblings, it was their turn to be heroes and to try to save the town. With all the help from the townspeople they could gather, they transformed themselves into men to be presented as the princes over the course of three days. Fet-Fruners was inspired watching their siblings explore who they were, both as heroes trying to save the town and as creative individuals expressing facets of who they were.

Mayor Florian did not want his children to leave but also knew that sometimes to be a hero—or to be the ally of a hero—you had to accept sacrifice and grant freedom to those you love. But before he'd let them go, he wanted to test their disguises to make sure they did not get caught for their ruse. He used his magician's powers on both, and both were quickly revealed to be princesses. Their plan was foiled.

Fet-Fruners realized they might be able to do what their sisters couldn't and began to work on becoming "Prince" Fet-Fruners. As Prince Fet-Fruners, he passed his father's magical tests and set off with the help of his own longtime companion horse, Murgu, whom Mayor Florian had granted the power to speak and guide Prince Fet-Fruners.

Along the way to the capital, Murgu shared everything he had learned over the years. He was a legendary horse who had taken part in the epic battles of warriors, leaders, and champions. All that Murgu shared helped the prince to be ready to serve as an epic hero.

Prince Fet-Fruners faced his first challenging battle before too long, when he came upon horrible monsters kidnapping children from local villages. The prince, with the help of Murgu, used his keen powers of observation, discovered the kidnappers' secret hideout, and with the help of the local army stopped the monsters once and for all. Everything began to fall into place for the prince. He felt more alive, at ease, calm, and whole than he ever had before.

Word of this arriving prince who defeated the evil monsters reached Emperor Coman. The emperor demanded that this prince perform one quest for him before being accepted as a part of the Royal Guard. Prince Fet-Fruners had to rescue Princess Iliane, a beautiful princess from another province, and bring her safely to Emperor Coman.

Princess Iliane was a clever and heroic adventurer of her own. However, her wisdom and heroic nature were not enough to keep her from being captured and held by an evil magical sorcerer. Prince Fet-Fruners, riding high on his string of heroic victories, confronted the sorcerer himself. Against the hand-to-hand combat skills the prince had been honing, the sorcerer's magic was not enough to prevent his defeat. Prince Fet-Fruners unlocked the castle chamber to rescue the beautiful Princess Iliane and return her to Emperor Coman's palace. As soon as they saw each other, they felt a spark.

On the journey back to the palace, Princess Iliane and Prince Fet-Fruners found themselves exchanging countless stories about where they grew up and about their families, whom they missed, as well as some of the heroic adventures they'd each had. They gabbed the entire way about life, love, and, of course, potatoes! Although the journey was long, they did not even have time to talk about how Princess Iliane had ended up captured.

As they approached the palace, Princess Iliane was struck silent. Prince Fet-Fruners hoped that her speechlessness was from the joy she felt at being freed and at being a guest at the palace, and he delivered her to the emperor.

Prince Fet-Fruners continued to perform other quests for the emperor but did not always feel that he was doing much good. He began to realize that being an epic hero meant fighting for all people and not just the emperor. Each time the prince rallied a local village to defeat an evil magician, a power-hungry creature, or a monster out to collect children, he felt like a real hero. The local villagers would thank him endlessly, and he loved bearing witness to their happiness, not only when they were granted freedom from their troubles, but also when he saw the joy they felt when they took part in fighting for a better world. Prince Fet-Fruners realized that his mission was to help people fight for the freedom to discover what made them happy and whole, just as he had.

Distracted by his heroic quests, Prince Fet-Fruners did not speak to Princess Iliane for some days. Then the emperor ordered Prince Fet-Fruners to retrieve a holy relic from an evil old wizard. The prince had stolen back artifacts that the emperor claimed were his many times before, always imagining that the treasure was going back to its rightful owner; he never questioned the emperor. But this quest was different. Not only did Prince Fet-Fruners doubt the emperor, but he wasn't sure the old wizard was even evil.

As a result, Prince Fet-Fruners was less stealthy than he'd been on earlier quests. His doubt made him pause and question each step. A thief—even a thief who thinks they are stealing for good—must move quickly to avoid being caught. Prince Fet-Fruners was not quick enough, and the wizard caught sight of the young hero just as he was escaping from the temple.

"I curse you, thief!" yelled the old wizard. "How dare you steal from me! I have served the good people of this village, and you serve no one but your corrupt emperor! Who do you think you are? You will no longer know who you are!"

Before the prince made it out of earshot, he heard the old wizard chant:

If you are a man, no longer shall you be,
If you are a woman, you are not she.
For I curse you with a change,
One intended to derange . . .
A reversal, a swap, a switch,
This curse on you will become your glitch!

Prince Fet-Fruners felt a change, and he knew serious magic was afoot. But it did not feel strange to him, or even like a glitch. Prince Fet-Fruners realized he was now a true prince—he had become a man—in every sense of the word! He felt whole. Despite the circumstances, the old wizard had actually given Prince Fet-Fruners a gift. Prince Fet-Fruners considered returning to the temple to thank the wizard but decided instead to get back to the palace. It was time to confront the emperor, after he dealt with the lingering heaviness in his heart.

Prince Fet-Fruners went to see Princess Iliane that evening, for the first time since her rescue.

"I am sorry I haven't seen you since we rode back here together," said the prince, sheepishly but warmly.

"I have been hearing the stories of your heroism here," replied the princess. "They are admirable, Fet-Fruners, but still you work for the emperor."

"I thought I was helping." The doubtful but newly self-confident hero sighed.

"I always knew the emperor was evil and power hungry," said the princess.

"Why didn't you tell me when we met?" asked the prince.

"We never got to it, swept up as we were in each other . . . and potatoes," she replied cheerfully. "And I assumed you knew. As his power has grown, he has taken more and more from villages. But he is guilty of more than just demanding taxes; he has monsters kidnapping children for his army. And now he has taken me, with your help. You simply moved me from one captor to another."

"I am sorry," said the prince, shocked and repentant. "I had no idea. I was shortsighted and wrong. I see how strong you are and what a heroic voice you have. On our journey, when you told me of your heroic deeds, was when I started to fall in love with you. I knew when you stopped speaking that something was wrong, but I convinced myself it was not."

"I started to feel something for you as well," confirmed the princess, "and yet I am never allowed to be free. Let us change that together."

So Prince Fet-Fruners and Princess Iliane set out with a plan. The prince called his father and sisters to the palace for help. Under the guise of coming to celebrate the emperor's victories—which they knew were in fact the prince's—they arrived at the palace, and the emperor remained distracted for the afternoon. Princess Iliane took this chance to see the Royal Guard. Through her fervent and impassioned appeal, Princess Iliane convinced the Royal Guard to see the emperor for what he was: a weak, power-hungry ruler who convinced others to help him keep power in spite of his own feebleness.

Although she was successful in convincing the second-in-command that he was serving a corrupt leader, Princess Iliane decided that the emperor was hers to overthrow. While the emperor was still distracted by Prince Fet-Fruners and his family, Princess Iliane attacked and defeated him. Through her own cunning wisdom and steadfast strength, Princess Iliane had freed the kingdom.

From then on, Princess Iliane and Prince Fet-Fruners presided over the kingdom. Their rule was known as one of hope and freedom. They allowed each village in the former empire to work together as they built a better world. The couple made sure they conferred that freedom—as well as love—on everyone in the kingdom, so that each person could find their way to being whole.

DAVID AND JONATHAN
ANCHOR EACH OTHER

Written in the sixth century BCE about a potentially real person who lived three hundred years earlier, this story is one of loyalty, love, and identity. As it comes from the Judeo-Christian Bible, in addition to being shared in some Muslim tales, it is one of the most studied of all myths. It is nearly impossible to separate the myth from the thousands of years of retellings. What all versions are clear on is that David and Jonathan are a true model of intimacy and love.

Prince Jonathan loved archery. Even as a spritely young child—the eldest sibling of nine—Jonathan was drawn to any activity that involved his bow and arrow. He loved the moment of standing and aiming the bow, pushing his reddish-brown hair behind his ears, and scrunching his eyelids over his wide brown eyes just before a shot. At that moment, it was just him and the target; the rest of the world faded away.

As a child, Jonathan spent hours each day with an archery teacher who helped him understand each aspect of the sport. The more Jonathan learned about archery, the more he loved it. His teacher helped him develop his stance (the strong way to stand firm while aiming) and encouraged him to understand the value of an anchor point—a position that each person finds for themselves, someplace on their face, where the bowstring is pulled back to before firing. This anchor point created consistency and stability as each archer developed their strength. Jonathan loved establishing his stance, honing his concentration, and choosing his anchor point every time.

As Jonathan grew older, he felt like the role of prince took him farther and farther away from his love of archery. His father, King Saul, would pull him away to demand he learn how some part of the kingdom worked, usually the army. Jonathan was only interested in the ways he could help train everyone to be stronger archers, particularly since he was too young to take part in battle. King Saul, meanwhile, was certain that their god was going to anoint Jonathan king after he was gone, as he was the eldest of all his children.

Full of swagger and self-importance, King Saul allowed his hubris to eventually lead him to defy his god's orders. King Saul's god had ordered that a captive enemy king be killed, but King Saul kept his prisoner alive and put him on display for the kingdom to see. It was not mercy that led King Saul to defy his god, but his desire to display his power over others. His arrogance led him to imagine that his and his family's places were set in stone, but they were not. Their deity not only had the power to alter the mortals' lives to his will but also had the willingness to do so. After this defiance, their god told King Saul that Jonathan was no longer to be the next ruler of the kingdom. A new successor to the throne would be found and would arrive in the kingdom imminently.

King Saul was outraged, and though he was already known quite well for his anger, he now felt a boiling fury he'd never felt before. King Saul's anger grew and grew as he waited every morning to meet whomever his god had selected to be the next king. However, once Jonathan heard the news, he started to feel a little lighter, even freer. He was finally able to get out and do what he wanted to; he chose to take a journey across the land. Jonathan planned to practice his archery, bringing his training to the small villages and helping others around him become stronger in their practice.

One day, while Jonathan was still away, the next chosen king arrived in the kingdom. David was a beautiful young man, with an entrancing smile, eyes that flickered so they appeared silver, and long, curly chestnut hair. Initially, as King Saul spent time with David, he enjoyed the young man's company. David was kind and generous. He was still uncertain whether the message that he was to become king—which he'd received from the heavens in a dream—was true, but he was excited to learn from King Saul as much as he could.

A shepherd throughout most of his childhood, David was also widely known for his musical ability. Not only could David sing, but he played the harp and entertained the king's court repeatedly. With each tune, King Saul found that the people around him were calmer, so he appointed David not just the armorer for the kingdom, but also the court musician.

David was too young to become a soldier, having just turned the same age as Jonathan, still a year away from being allowed to fight in battle. But that didn't stop him from his legendary confrontation with the giant Goliath. Armed with only his slingshot, David felled Goliath, and his victory brought him endless attention.

King Saul wanted to shower David with rewards. He invited the boy to join his family, perhaps by beginning a relationship with one of his daughters. David was not interested and refused. Instead, King Saul made him commander of the army, despite his young age. For the special celebration honoring David, Jonathan decided to come home and meet the young man he had heard so much about.

While the castle often felt oppressive to him, Jonathan finally looked forward to returning. Upon his arrival, Jonathan decided to check in on the future king. He opened the gate to David's quarters and immediately felt like he did in that moment right before he took a shot with his bow and arrow.

It was as if everything melted away, everything disappeared, and all he could see was David. All that existed was David and him. Before he even heard David's voice, Jonathan felt like David was inside his head and heart, as if their spirits had known each other before.

Over the next few months, Jonathan stayed in the kingdom to spend as much time as he could with David. At first, Jonathan wasn't sure if the giant-slaying shepherd shared his feelings, but the more time they spent together, the more Jonathan was certain the attraction was mutual. Soon, they were deeply in love. Jonathan even taught David his love of archery and, naturally, David was a quick learner.

Considering that David was next in line for his throne, King Saul decided to put him through test after test, sometimes sending him out on strange quests. But each time, David was successful, and this enraged the king. It made David's existence in the kingdom quite volatile, with little stability to stay grounded upon, except Jonathan.

One day, King Saul tried to get Jonathan to turn against David. He begged and pleaded, hoping to convince Jonathan that by removing David from the kingdom, perhaps he would be restored as the successor to the throne. But Jonathan knew that the strongest stance he could take, the firmest ground on which he could stand, was to remain loyal to his love. He refused his father, and his love for David calmed King Saul down . . . for a brief time.

A few peaceful months passed with King Saul, until things took a turn for the worse: the king became violent and attempted to kill both David and Jonathan in a moment of misguided rage. While the king's attempted murder failed—his spear stuck in a wall, missing the couple—the pair quickly realized that it would not be safe for them to remain together in the kingdom.

David and Jonathan swore their loyalty to each other, promising to protect each other. But Jonathan knew that David was the one who needed more protection, despite their mutual love.

"Let me be your anchor," Jonathan told David. "I can be the place where we are steadied. You can always return to our love, but I fear you need to go. Our bond is secure, always, and let that bring you strength. I can continue to make sure you are safe from here. We have forged this sacred bond, and I believe in that."

"As do I, love," responded David, his reply affectionate but exasperated. "I know that you make me stronger, and I know that we have this love, but I also know that I cannot be without you. Please, I beg, do not make us part."

"Let us try," pleaded Jonathan. "Our love and faith are enough. And if you let me anchor you while you stay safe, one day you can be the best king there ever was."

David refused to leave the kingdom but promised he would take care of himself, and Jonathan agreed to let them try. But tensions escalated, and finally David decided to confront and fight King Saul, with a blade in hand. David chose mercy, as he always did, and used his blade to simply cut a small part of the king's robes instead of harming him. This kindness calmed King Saul, who promised goodwill toward them both. But Jonathan felt sure this would not be the end.

A few days later, Jonathan learned that his father's erratic temper was raging again and he would no longer be keeping the promise he'd made. David was in immediate danger. The couple decided that David would head out into the forest to hide, and Jonathan would deceive King Saul into believing that he had gone back to his home village.

It was a most difficult goodbye. Even though they had known each other for hardly a year, they had grown accustomed to being together every day. They shared a kiss and wept as they parted. And for some time, their plan worked. The two would meet in clandestine encounters in the woods whenever Jonathan was sure he was not being followed and it was safe for them to be together.

As King Saul's rage escalated, even in David's absence, so too did the battles across the land. The conflicts grew so numerous that the king demanded that every capable person be a part of the army. Jonathan was pleased to finally bring his archery skills to battle, though he feared being away from David. Jonathan and David got together in the forest one final time before battle. Under the canopy of trees, they reinforced their sacred bond and reiterated their love for and loyalty to each other.

"Jonathan," David began, "your love has kept me safe. You have steadied me, and you have kept us steadied in the most outrageous of circumstances. I would not be alive without you. I would not know what it is to love without you. I would not be able to be a king without you."

"David, my love, we are forever in a covenant," Jonathan replied. "No matter what happens, I know that you are stronger because our love has been our ballast. Even in spirit, absent each other, my love will remain an anchor to you. Return to this for stability and strength."

King Saul and his children who fought beside him—including Jonathan—were all killed in battle. After King Saul died, David learned the tragic news. For days and days, David wept for his loss. As he finally took the throne, he called out to the heavens, "Jonathan, my love. Your love has surpassed all other love there is. No other love I have felt or will feel compares to you, and I serve this kingdom and our god in the name of that love." Thus began King David's reign over the kingdom.

HYACINTHUS AND APOLLO
ACCEPT LOVE AND LOSS

The Greek myth of Hyacinthus and Apollo has been written and rewritten countless times since it was first recorded around the year 168 CE. With variations in each telling, Hyacinthus's relationship with his boyfriend Thamyris remains one of the oldest recorded tales of gay love in Greek mythology, where their love is known as the first gay love. It is Apollo's tribute to his love for Hyacinthus that persists eternally.

The Spartan prince Hyacinthus was known across the land as soon as he was born. He was the child of a muse—a god that inspired mortals—named Clio and a mortal king called Pierus. Hyacinthus was a charismatic child, with bright, golden locks of hair that curled and curved into shiny flaxen spirals. He smiled and smirked, and his eyes conveyed cleverness. Hyacinthus was always peaceful, clear, and steady, and everyone around him felt a magnetic draw to his aura of calm, overcome with the feeling of ease created by his entrancing looks and personality.

As Hyacinthus grew older, these qualities amplified and deepened, becoming an irresistible and intoxicating allure. Hyacinthus was simply gorgeous, and everyone he encountered felt his beauty, charm, and gentleness, including his first boyfriend, the singer Thamyris.

Thamyris loved Hyacinthus, though unfortunately more than Hyacinthus loved him. He wrote songs about Hyacinthus and performed them far and wide. Thamyris regularly triumphed in song competitions with his

beautiful melodies, but there was one competition that Thamyris lost: the one for Hyacinthus's heart. When competing against the gods themselves for Hyacinthus's love, it was no contest.

As the wind blew through Hyacinthus's golden locks, he felt the warm breeze down his neck of Zephyrus, god of the west wind, and later that of Boreas, god of the north wind. But neither wind god could compare to his greatest love: the bright and shining star Apollo, god of the sun.

Apollo first spotted Hyacinthus when the rays of the bright yellow sun—the very sun Apollo gifted to mortals—reflected in Hyacinthus's golden hair and in his sparkling eyes.

"Hyacinthus, your beauty both inside and out shines more brightly than any light I can shed upon mortals from the sun or the stars," Apollo said.

Apollo soon became the true love of Hyacinthus. In turn, Apollo loved Hyacinthus more than anyone he had ever known. He wrote and recited poetry for Hyacinthus—verses upon verses that celebrated the clever, gentle, beautiful Hyacinthus and the love they shared. Apollo even left behind his home in Delphi to be with Hyacinthus.

Everything they did together was filled with joy and created more light—and love—wherever they went. Apollo taught Hyacinthus how to use the bow and arrow. Apollo was, after all, also the god of archery. Hyacinthus was thoroughly invested in preserving nature and the beauty of the world around him, so they never hunted. Archery instead became a sport of play for them. And archery was not the only sport they engaged in. They found all manner of physical exercise—boxing, wrestling, gymnastics—to be just another thing they could share.

They also created music together. On the lyre, a melodic and beautiful stringed instrument, their poems, stories, and lyrics came alive. All who heard their songs felt the undying, eternal love they shared. But would their love be eternal? They both wanted to know, and Apollo—who somehow also found time to be the god of oracles—helped Hyacinthus learn the practice of divination. He spent each night showing his partner the methods that seers used to understand the world and determine where it was going next.

When Hyacinthus tried to see what was to come for the world, himself, and Apollo, he discovered that the bright light of love he felt was blotted out and dark. He could not see what was next. The darkness was in fact a terrible, tragic ending coming all too soon.

A few days later, Apollo and Hyacinthus were amusing themselves in an open field, tossing a discus. (The discus throw was a way that mortals honored the almighty gods through sport at the Olympics.) The bronze discus was polished so smooth that it reflected the light of the day and very nearly looked golden as it shone. Hyacinthus and Apollo laughed as they flung it here and there. They felt the warm glow of the sun, their love, and their life spent together. Suddenly, a terrible accident occurred. The wind caught the discus in just the wrong way, tilting it so the sun reflected off its shiny surface. Hyacinthus was momentarily blinded by the sun's reflection, and the discus fatally struck him in the head.

Hyacinthus lay dying in the field, under the bright, blinding sun and the warm glow of Apollo, who held his body. Apollo had but a moment to say goodbye to his love. Hyacinthus could barely speak, but Apollo—quickly losing his golden luster—was able to sing to him.

> *You made my life whole with your loving glow,*
> *But I can never be a mortal, that is something I regretfully know.*
> *You shall live forever on my lips, my tongue, my heart,*
> *And I plead to the gods for the moment we may rejoin and*
> *never part.*

Despite Apollo's pleas to the other gods, he could not become a mortal to be with his love, nor could he turn Hyacinthus immortal.

"Aiiiiiii," Apollo wailed. "Aiiiiiii," he called in his grief.

Hyacinthus continued to fade, his blood seeping into the field around him. Apollo's grief was so mighty that out of the blood suddenly appeared bright purple flowers, their color so bright, so vibrant, that it warmed Apollo's spirit. And each petal of the beautiful, magical flowers appeared to be marked with "ai, ai," the words of Apollo's powerful cry. It was the love and grief of Apollo that resurrected Hyacinthus in this flower. Forevermore, the hyacinth flower represented the cycle of mortality—of death and resurrection—and the power of love that brings the pain of loss alongside it.

LAKAPATI CULTIVATES PROSPERITY

This creation myth is part of the Tagalog and Filipino canon. While not written down until the sixteenth century, the story likely goes back hundreds of years, if not more. The gods who are part of this story continue to be celebrated, not just for the ways they affect the universe and help all beings, but as an inspiration for the committed love they share.

The most benevolent of all the deities was the beautiful goddess Lakapati. She existed before the creation of the world. She was the goddess of prosperity and harvest, always known for her giving nature. Like the cornstalks of the harvest, she was tall and slender, with her long, soft hair as satiny as the corn silk. She always stood upright—standing boldly and bravely for what she believed in, as Lakapati was also openly and proudly transgender.

Lakapati's name was a core part of her identity—it meant "giver of the world," a flashy but ultimately earned title for all that she gave. She wanted to make sure every being could be themselves, and their best selves at that. It was through her love that she gave so much, and Lakapati had two great loves.

The Earth was born through Lakapati's first love. Before the Earth was formed, the gods resided in a field of the heavens, where Lakapati met and fell in love with Bathala, an intersex, transgender deity looking for their own place in the universe. The two lived together happily, though Bathala was always searching for their purpose and sometimes grew envious that Lakapati's compassion gave her something on which to focus. Bathala decided it was time to find something they could be passionate about too.

Lakapati loved to explore the fields of the heavens, as she was goddess of the harvest. On one expedition she found a unique and exquisite banana plant. Lakapati had the idea to combine it with some clay and give it to Bathala so that they could create something with it. Bathala loved the gifts and started to experiment, eventually transforming the banana plant and the clay into mountains, oceans, and land. Thus, Bathala created the Earth, and so Bathala became known as the creator of all things, taking their earned place as the god of all gods. Their new role and responsibilities became Bathala's priority and, with Lakapati focused on her own cultivation, the couple decided to end their time together and go their separate ways.

Lakapati continued to explore in the fields of the gods, finding new ways to bring prosperity to all beings on the newly formed Earth. While traveling through the fields one day, she encountered Mapulon, god of the seasons and health. He also provided the rain and the warmth to the Earth, so that the land could flourish. He was stunning and widely known as the most beautiful of the gods. Mapulon confessed to Lakapati that he'd loved her from afar for some time but never wanted to get between her and Bathala. With Bathala out of the picture, Mapulon and Lakapati could be together. They discovered that, working together, they could make the land fertile for harvest. As the two worked more and more closely together, they became known as the providers for all beings.

Lakapati and Mapulon also loved having their own fun. They danced through the fields of the gods, often in lavish costumes. Mapulon had always been known for wearing masks. With the changing of each season, Mapulon wore a different mask to represent the season. For Mapulon, the seasons represented balance, with summer's glow counteracting winter's frigidity, and spring creating harmony with fall. As Lakapati and Mapulon worked together to provide rain and a bountiful harvest, they had to find balance just as the weather did. They knew that after a drought, a raging storm must come.

Mapulon was, in fact, created as two aspects in one god. He'd always felt that he had two selves, and regulating the seasons helped him understand how that was a strength. Lakapati had also long felt this way. She had broken boundaries to feel whole, fusing together many parts of herself.

Lakapati and Mapulon became inseparable, perfectly balanced always. Just as the seasons provided what the land needed for harvest, their love provided each with sustenance. Lakapati and Mapulon lived together, balancing the Earth's ecosystem.

Their balance provided the Earth with resources, and their love provided it with beauty. The couple had a child together, Anagolay, goddess of lost things. Anagolay helped people find what they needed—just as her parents had found not only themselves, but each other.

LAN CAIHE AND THEIR JADE CASTANETS

The stories of Lan Caihe and the eight immortals likely do not refer to real people, but they were written as if they were histories. These Taoist Chinese stories first began appearing in the 1100s CE, though the events they purport to relate took place in the 600s to 800s. The thousand-year-old tales embrace the queerness of Lan Caihe in their family; indeed, plenty of stories— such as this one—are not even about their identity, rendering their queerness as a normal part of the epic myths.

Lan Caihe was one of eight siblings—the eight immortals—and that created a lot of expectations for them. For Lan Caihe and their sisters and brothers to become immortal, they had to prove to the gods just how exceptional they were. In different ways, through fantastic feats, each of them demonstrated why they were deserving, and the gods elevated them from the mortal plane, granting them powers in the process. From the time they became immortal, they were the subjects of stories about who they could be, who they should be, and who they should not be. Each time these stories were retold, it felt like a cage of expectations was closing in on Lan Caihe.

Lan Caihe always knew that they did not share the gender of their sister or that of their brothers. It was not just the way Lan Caihe expressed who they were; they were uncomfortable with a binary set of expectations. Lan Caihe possessed a deeper feeling inside, a sense of who they were and how they related to the world that was profoundly different from the binary.

For Lan Caihe, identity was fluid. Sometimes Lan Caihe was what some people might label or identify as male. Sometimes Lan Caihe could be called female. And sometimes Lan Caihe was a combination of the two, or even neither. And so Lan Caihe chose a non-binary gender identity.

When Lan Caihe was still a human, they were a musician. They wandered from town to city, coast to coast, sharing their love of music and dancing. They were known for performing with a pair of jade castanets, which were small clappers usually made from wood, but in this case from bright green jade stone. The castanets were a gift from a close mentor who taught Lan Caihe music. With their movement and sound, Lan Caihe brought the castanets' effusive joy alive for an audience. When Lan Caihe became immortal, they discovered that each sibling had a single object of the most importance to them. For Lan Caihe it was those bright-green castanets that mattered the most, much to the chagrin of their siblings, who had to listen to the music all day, every day!

Any sound—such as the sound of passing horses—was just the start of a song that flowed out of Lan Caihe. They tapped their feet, stomped, danced, and clapped their green jade castanets. Lan Caihe heard so many sounds in nature's tune that were music to their ears—birds became a symphony; breezes rustling trees became an orchestra. They started to dance and stomp so much that they found it easier to wear just one shoe, so that with one foot they could stomp their boot to the beat, while with their other foot they could dance on the bare earth.

One day, Lan Caihe and their siblings all decided to find a way they could use their most cherished objects to show off their powers and glide over the ocean. Having already surfed the clouds and the wind as a family of immortals, the siblings felt that gliding over the water was thrilling and exciting in whole new ways. While the plan was not hatched to get rid of the noise-making castanets, a few of Lan Caihe's siblings would not have minded if they were lost at sea during the adventure!

With years of experience in all manners of dancing, Lan Caihe was able to easily, expertly dance on the jade clappers. The tiny green instruments became a small surfboard of sorts for Lan Caihe to sail over the ocean's surface. The music of the ocean waves crashing and moving was a thrill in itself for Lan Caihe.

Wrapped up in the new symphony of the waves and ocean creatures, Lan Caihe failed to notice the Dragon King of the Eastern Sea approaching. Though dragons were not known for their stealth, Lan Caihe was distracted by the music in their mind. Suddenly the Dragon King swept up Lan Caihe and their clappers and took them back to his palace as a way to punish the family of immortals for playing in his kingdom.

To help save Lan Caihe, their siblings sought the help of many other dragons who were unhappy with the Dragon King's decision to fight the immortals. An intense battle quickly ensued. Heroic dragons lost their lives trying to return Lan Caihe to their siblings. With the help—and sacrifice—of the kind dragons, the battle was won. The Dragon King agreed to give back Lan Caihe and remain in his kingdom, leaving everyone else unbothered. Thanks to the immortals and the heroic dragons working together, the evil Dragon King even agreed to leave them all alone if they crossed into his domain again.

In exchange for their aid and their sacrifice, to express their appreciation for being saved, Lan Caihe gave up their most prized possession—the jade clappers—as a gift to the dragon clan who helped. For even the most treasured object could not compare to the importance of working together, and the way the heroic alliance between the immortals and the dragons had saved Lan Caihe.

PHILOCTETES AND HERCULES HOLD ON

❧

The Greco-Roman story of Philoctetes and Hercules (also known in Greek stories as Heracles) is not the most famous of the hero's myths. As with most Greek- or Roman-originating myths, it comes from well before the current era, possibly the seventh century BCE, though oral tradition predated that. This story depicts a deep, abiding love, and how that love became a part of a heroic victory.

Philoctetes the philosopher was of average height and dark-skinned, with striking black hair atop his head and spread over his body, including his closely connected, thick, prominent eyebrows. His name primarily meant "a love of possessions." Known for his good sense throughout his childhood, Philoctetes was also a collector and a thinker who had a mighty heart. With that heart, he loved and loved, more than just objects as his name indicated.

Philoctetes and Hercules, the half-god adventurer, met when they were young during a chance encounter before the mighty hero's famed twelve labors. Over a short time, it became clear to Philoctetes that he loved Hercules, and the love was reciprocal, though he knew that the love wouldn't last. Hercules had already had many loves in his life—of all genders—and Philoctetes believed their relationship was likely to pass as quickly as the breeze moved through the trees. But just as even a momentary breeze carrying a sweet floral scent could ignite the senses, Hercules ignited the passions of Philoctetes, and they became a couple.

While Philoctetes was correct that their love wouldn't last, Hercules never betrayed him, and the two continued to feel a spark and remain connected even after moving on from their time together. A few years later, Hercules and Deianeira, a Calydonian princess, were married, though it was to be yet another brief relationship for the demigod, thanks in part to his betrayal.

Deianeira discovered that Hercules had deceived her and decided to use a magic lotion that would control Hercules and prevent further lying. Unbeknownst to her, the magical relic she was given turned out to be a deadly poison. Hercules also discovered this too late and was faced with his slow but inevitable death, which he of course wished to avoid.

Hercules hoped the gods would honor his feats of strength and bring him to Mount Olympus, but to be made immortal he'd ironically need to die first, and the gods of Mount Olympus would not permit him to take his own life. Despite his betrayal of so many people he loved, including Deianeira, Hercules could not find anyone who was willing to help him sacrifice himself, including his hurt, estranged wife. He turned to his former love Philoctetes, who was reluctant but willing to grant Hercules the mercy that no other would offer.

Before Philoctetes could light the flames of the funeral pyre onto which Hercules climbed, he asked the dying demigod for a gift—any trinket he could possess to remember him by. Hercules remembered that Philoctetes had always loved shooting with a bow and arrow. The thinker found the precision and lightness of the arrow to be remarkable, though his love of nature meant he never used it to take a life. Ironically, here Philoctetes was, taking the life of his first love, but at least he would have something to hold on to.

Hercules granted his love, Philoctetes, his famed bow and arrow. With sorrow in his heart and a heaviness in his soul, Philoctetes lit the funeral pyre for his lover. He then ran away, wanting to be far from the sight of Hercules perishing. As he ran, eyes filled with tears and unable to see the rocky path in front of him, he stumbled and injured his foot.

Thanks to Philoctetes's act of love and mercy, Hercules was indeed brought to Mount Olympus and became the god of strength and heroes. As a deity, however, Hercules could no longer contact Philoctetes or any other mortal. He would have to remain at a distance.

Philoctetes moved to the beautiful but isolated island of Lemnos to tend to his injuries—both his foot and his grieving heart. Years passed as Philoctetes resided on the island, alone and sorrowful. However, he was surrounded by the objects he loved, including Hercules's bow and arrows, which never missed. The magical, careful flight each arrow took gave Philoctetes some comfort, reminding him of the breeze on his face that was Hercules's breath as they whispered of their love to each other. He felt a little better each time he remembered.

Outside of Lemnos, the world continued to be a place of betrayal, loss, and death. Philoctetes was glad to be removed from the Trojan War. When the mysterious and soon-to-be legendary Odysseus, the fabled Greek king, came to the island of Lemnos, Philoctetes wanted simply to be left alone with the things he loved.

Odysseus sought Hercules's bow and arrow, however, and was prepared to do anything to get them. The king and his army had been told by a seer that this bow and arrow were the only way they'd win the war. They tried to explain this to Philoctetes, who would barely listen, unable to imagine parting with Hercules's gift.

Philoctetes would not help them. But as the soldiers began to leave, Philoctetes saw a flash of light behind his home and ran back to see if something was aflame. Instead, he found Hercules, as clear as day, appearing from Mount Olympus.

"My dear love, Philoctetes," said Hercules, his voice like the hum of the breeze moving through the trees. Philoctetes was speechless, startled by this vision of the man he'd missed every day for a decade.

"It is me, I am here, and I am sorry I could not come to you sooner. It is in this moment of crisis among our people that I can come to you, and I must be brief," he continued. "I know you are holding on to that bow because of me. I know you love me every day still, and you must know that I also love you."

"I cannot part with this final piece of you I have," said Philoctetes. "My parents named me after someone who loves things, and I love this thing most of all because it reminds me of you, and of us."

"I know you love these things you can touch, you can explore, you can have, and you can hold. I am not any of those things anymore, but I still am something you can think of, remember, and reflect upon. But I am not that bow. We are not in that bow. We are in here," Hercules said as his apparition reached out toward Philoctetes's heart. "And here," he continued as he moved his hand toward Philoctetes's head.

"I know that, Hercules, I know that," Philoctetes said tearfully, "but it was so hard to get over what happened, and the only thing that helped me through was firing that bow and arrow every day and listening to its buzz on the wind, feeling the breeze on my face," Philoctetes pleaded.

"Our love exists whether you fire that bow and arrow or not. Our love exists whether you move on to another love or not. Our love exists for all time and always, because it lives in our hearts and our minds, and it lives in the stories we tell. On Mount Olympus, my love for you is known. And if you become a part of this moment for our people, our story will be known and will live on forever, and you can live on too, healed and whole," Hercules explained.

Philoctetes, lover of things, also loved stories. He believed everything Hercules said to be true. The pair embraced and kissed before Hercules departed the mortal Earth once again. Philoctetes returned to Odysseus and his soldiers, and joined them, with the famed bow and arrow.

Philoctetes fought in the Trojan War and became a hero. He even participated in the famed Trojan horse attack. He continued his life after the war, traveling from city to city. And each place he went, the memory of his legendary partner, Hercules the strong, always followed him, with the story of their unbreakable love.

SEDNA FINDS FREEDOM IN THE WATER

The Inuit people of Alaska, Canada, Siberia, and Greenland are culturally similar Indigenous people. Their myths—including that of the goddess Sedna and her sacrifice—may date back to as early as the year 1000 BCE. Not only is this tale of Sedna a creation myth for so much of life in the sea, but it is also a story of inner strength, breaking free, and finding love.

Sedna felt like so many other daughters did—she just could not do anything right in her parents' eyes. Even as an adult, Sedna always felt like a child at home.

Sedna and her parents lived in the icy north. They had always lived on glaciers and over the vast, cold ocean. Since she was born, Sedna had known the beauty and power of water. Her life had been split between the ice of the frozen water and the deep, vast, ever-changing sea.

Sedna's father was a broad man with deep wrinkles. He lived a long life full of hunting and exploration, but only near their home—never farther. Her mother was a tall, beautiful person with white hair so bright that it glowed. She was also a hunter, always efficient and taking great care to use precision in her craft. Among her neighbors in the village, she was known for being a perfectionist.

Both of Sedna's parents were constantly overbearing and controlling, not at a loss to find things for which to criticize her.

"Sedna, why does your hair look like that?" her mother asked.

"Sedna, why do you spend time with that friend?" she questioned.

"Sedna, why are you wearing all those rings on your fingers?" she demanded.

"Sedna, why do you insist on being this way?" she said sharply.

Her father was the crueler of the pair, and his cruelty seemed to have worsened as she grew older.

"Sedna, I wish you were not the way you are," her father sniped.

"Sedna, I wish you were more like your brother," he challenged.

"Sedna, I wish you were a boy," he said ruthlessly.

"Sedna, I wish you were not born," he complained callously.

Her parents' expectations for Sedna's life became demands—where she should go, whom she should speak to, even whom she should marry. In response, Sedna, with her dark, matted hair; her broad, firm shoulders; and her long, ringed fingers, continued to do what she wanted. But every little question, every demand, and every cruel word weighed her down, making her feel heavy enough to sink through the ice.

Sedna felt an affinity for water. It conformed as it slid and moved through the rivers and cut the cliffs. Water also resisted as it knocked against the shores. Water could be both the hardest, when it was jagged ice, and the softest, when it was freshly fallen snow. It was all-consuming during storms and floods, but also life-giving as it quenched the thirst of travelers on long journeys. Sedna's fascination with water led her to take journeys on her own throughout the tundra. Much to the irritation of her family, particularly her father, Sedna ventured out, sometimes for days at a time.

On one journey, Sedna discovered and quickly fell in love with a bird. It was a beautiful, majestic, midnight-black bird of prey with a massive wingspan. The bird couldn't question her hairstyle or jewelry choices! As it flew it looked like a segment of the sky—devoid of all stars—was blackening with tar.

Sedna followed the bird for days. She watched where it nested and how it took care of itself and the other birds in the nest. She listened to its call and the flap of its wings. She witnessed as the moonlight occasionally caught a shiny feather and sparkle, like a diamond floating in the black sea.

By the time she returned home, a massive storm had brought rain and thunder upon her family home. The storm was pounding and ferocious. Rather than being concerned for Sedna's whereabouts and well-being, her family instead criticized her. Her father could not understand why she was gone for so long, or how a bird—or any animal for that matter—could be worth so much attention.

"How is this possible, Sedna?" he insisted, as if there were an answer that could satisfy him.

"I found beauty in the world of animals, Papa," Sedna pleaded. "The beauty of a creature free to make their own choices and free to fly their own way."

The fight continued for what felt like hours, until Sedna announced she was leaving.

"Go, then. Go fly away," said her father as Sedna set herself afloat in a small canoe on the wild, blackened ocean. The storm in Sedna's heart began raging as fiercely as the one in the sky.

The rainstorm got worse and worse.

The sky grew blacker and blacker.

The rain fell harder and harder.

The sea stirred wilder and wilder.

And the cold set in.

The canoe could no longer withstand the ocean's violence, and it flipped over. Sedna struggled to stay above the dark, ferocious waters. She felt the weight of herself falling, but she held on to the edge of the canoe.

Her fingers gripped the edge, her rings flashing as they reflected the streaks of lightning in the sky.

Sedna held on for as long as she could under the pounding rain and arctic wind. Hours passed as Sedna floated. Her frostbitten fingers began to freeze to the canoe. And as her heaviness finally began to pull her underwater, her fingers broke from her hands and she drifted down, down. The lightning flashed, the thunder boomed, and the water swallowed her whole.

The sea brought not death, but rescue. The dark, heavy, wild water transformed Sedna. She became a mighty goddess, the Mother of the Sea. With newfound goddess eyes, she took in the majesty of the sea life around her—the whales, seals, and so many other beautiful creatures. Each finger she had lost to the ravages of the ice was magically transformed into a species of sea creature, creating majestic giants of the sea.

Sedna settled into her new role with ease—even having fingers that became seals was a welcome change! Sometimes she missed her family, but she knew her family did not miss her. She felt more at home at the bottom of the sea than she ever did on land. Down there, she could resist the flow and control the current.

One day, Sedna encountered Qailertetang, the goddess of hunters, animals, and the weather. Qailertetang was a large woman, with black and silver hair that sparkled as it moved in the ocean's currents, and a broad, flat nose that spotlighted her beautiful face. It was almost as if her hair was the current itself, flowing and forming beautiful shapes around her, and her face was so stunning it was like the beautiful sparkling glints of reflected sun striking the water.

As Qailertetang spoke to Sedna, her voice carried on the waves of the ocean like a whisper. It electrified Sedna as she heard it.

"I brought you to me, you know," said Qailertetang.

"How is that possible?" asked Sedna.

"The storm was not my doing; I would never compel you to become the Mother of the Sea. But I saw you that night and believed I could save you. I implored the thunder and lightning to send you an undertow, knowing the ocean would claim you as their mother goddess. Look at what you have become."

"Look at what my fingers have become!" Sedna exclaimed, as the two laughed together.

Sedna and Qailertetang slowly fell in love over time. Sedna felt lighter and freer. Despite being below the surface of the ocean, Sedna knew it was her choice to love Qailertetang and remain a goddess. With the whales and seals that were born of Sedna's fingers, and with all the other wonderful sea creatures, they lived together on the ocean floor. Sedna and Qailertetang were known as the fiercely independent lovers that protected the ocean, the sky, the animals, and the humans who needed them all.

XOCHIPILLI CELEBRATES BEAUTY AND PLEASURE

This Aztec myth was shared in central Mexico during the 1300s CE. The oral tradition including elements of this story predates the Aztec tale among Indigenous peoples by generations. As a result of these stories, Xochipilli is still considered the patron god of queer men, and ancient statues and other depictions abound in central Mexico, illustrating his flamboyant appearance and honoring his love of pleasure for all.

A handsome young man and his beautiful girlfriend—whose names have been lost to time—loved to party and were always experimenting with sensations, trying out different foods, drinks, and flavors. They were interested in exploring the senses and appreciated the mortal bodies that allowed them to play with all their senses—touch, taste, smell, sight, and sound.

One day, the pair discovered an intoxicatingly delicious new drink—some combination of fruits—and decided to offer it to the gods. The gods appreciated it so much, they made the young man a god himself, and he left his lover behind to live her mortal life.

The man was christened Xochipilli, the beautiful god of pleasure. He was grateful to the other gods for giving him power. But before he could enhance, support, rule over, and guide the people who worshipped him and his new siblings, he had to look the part.

Xochipilli put together the most lavish, bright, colorful, and striking ensemble he could. At all times he wore a bird mask—but not just one mask, no. Xochipilli had many, many masks, nearly one for every day, so that he could present different colors, styles, and plumage. Underneath each mask was a coordinated crest of feathers, like a shawl or cape made of thousands of feathers—found, not farmed, of course, so as not to harm any animals. His staff, taller than he and helpful in both generating and commanding attention, was made of thousands of flowers. Each flower had its own shape and color, making the staff alone mesmerizing. And throughout his look, Xochipilli had butterflies. These beautiful mariposas (Spanish for "butterflies") were painted on his face and on his dark brown skin and inscribed on or otherwise embellished his clothing.

Xochipilli's look immediately told his followers what he was the god of: flowers, artists, dance, music, and pleasure. All these things together made him the colorful deity of artistic sensibilities.

The people who worshipped Xochipilli and the other gods were living in a society of much aggression and upheaval. For these followers, it became hard to imagine any other way of being. There was so much violence and suffering. Much of the violence was at the hands of misguided leaders who saw aggression as strength, and this sensibility was encoded into their sense of gender too. Men were always expressing their belief that they were meant to be dominant through their superior nature and that they were also entitled to violence. Eventually everyone of all gender identities started to believe this must be nature.

Xochipilli did not follow this belief. He was interested in the fluid nature of gender, which was also part of his domain. He cared not for labels and restrictions, nor for expectations and norms. His focus on pleasure and artistic creation led him to challenge the way things were and to create change. He was also the god of same-sex love and passion, all part of the way that he challenged expectations.

Xochipilli was relaxed about life. He was interested in pleasure. However, he was also keenly aware that one person's pleasure could affect the pleasure of another. He knew that just because he enjoyed a particular type of flower did not mean he could harvest all those flowers. Or just because he liked a particular type of bird, that did not mean he could keep the bird caged. Or just because he enjoyed one type of music and another god or mortal enjoyed another, that he had any right to say his was better. As a true god of good feelings and with a pure love of all living things, he wanted everyone to be able to support their own and one another's passions and joys.

Xochipilli was joined by a god twin named Xochiquetzal, who oversaw love and beauty. She also oversaw flowers and the pleasure of the senses, working closely with her brother to make sure all genders, particularly women, were supported in expressing their passions and pleasures. She also oversaw crafting and creation, including childbirth.

Together, Xochipilli and Xochiquetzal lived in Tamoanchan, a mythical paradise high in the skies that could only be accessed by climbing a single, huge flowering tree that never went out of bloom, growing out of a hidden spot on Earth. Xochiquetzal was born in Tamoanchan, so the entire misty paradise was imbued with feminine energy and beautiful accessories, and the two loved being there as they planned how they would bring more beauty, more pleasure, and more love into the world.

The souls of artists came to Tamoanchan between their lifetimes, to commingle with one another, to feel inspired by the beauty, and to connect with their gods Xochipilli and Xochiquetzal. Each soul spent time in Tamoanchan to refresh and explore. As the soul began another life as a mortal, they took that passion back with them to experiment. Whatever that source of passion and pleasure was, each soul sought to express it, with themselves and with their community. Pleasure and beauty became a driving force of the world, offering a glimmer of hope that the lean toward aggression and violence, particularly among the most powerful mortals, would pass if each person could find their passions and express their loves.

LOKI DEFIES
RIGID BOUNDARIES

Loki has quickly become one of the most well-known—perhaps the most famous—of the Norse gods. Part of Scandinavian mythology, Loki's stories were composed in writing during the thirteenth century, though they all predate this as an oral tradition, possibly dating to 500 BCE. These stories persist because of the values that they place on broad-mindedness and the importance of challenging people to open their minds and their hearts.

Loki knew how to adapt to any situation. Some might call it being flexible—and others might think it's trickery or slipperiness—but Loki's adaptability manifested as an actual shape-shifting ability. Some of this trickiness was helped by just how handsome Loki was, as well as how cunningly his mind worked. Adapting constantly to your surroundings could be beautiful and could create diversity, but could also be challenging and traumatic.

Loki's choices meant that he was continually known as a trickster god, and many associated him with mischief, despite those moments being exceptions for him. While his choices often led him to assist his fellow gods, the stories that stuck about him were the ones in which he was unpredictable, or even chaotic.

Often Loki was called ergi, an Old Norse term indicating one who defies boundaries in any number of ways, but especially gender. Breaking with norms was ergi. It was also Loki's goal. Loki wanted to push everyone's boundaries. He wanted all of society, which he felt a responsibility

to support as one of the gods, to break more rules. Loki did not have any malicious intent; he was pushing for greater openness and understanding.

Loki's shifting nature helped him to express what he valued above all else: fluidity. For him, gender and sexuality were deeply fluid. While for some of his fellow gods these identities were firmly fixed—as for Thor, the god of thunder and Loki's brother, being male; or Sif, goddess of the harvest and Thor's onetime wife, being heterosexual—for Loki it never made sense to be just one thing.

When Loki was younger, he tried learning all the magic he could. While sorcery itself was frowned upon by his fellow gods, he knew that he needed to become an expert in everything to prove his capability. Only once he became an expert could he be sure that any criticism, any attacks on his character, would be outweighed by just how skillful he was.

Loki knew that for the gods, consuming the heart of something was one way to embody or become it—to truly take in everything that was a part of that being's essence, including their wisdom. While born male, Loki wanted to absorb everything related to feminine magic, traditionally taught only to women. He sought out a hidden cave that contained the heart of a sorceress who had long since died.

Holding his nose and closing his eyes, Loki swallowed the heart and was instantly overwhelmed with feeling. His entire being changed in that moment. It was not the first time Loki—now a woman—had shape-shifted, and it surely would not be the last, but it was magical. Suddenly insights about magic, sorcery, the earth, and all things feminine came into Loki's essence, merging, mixing, and muddying the boundaries that *she* had previously felt.

One act of creation magic was pregnancy. While embodying the sorceress and with nothing but her magical thoughts, Loki made herself pregnant and gave birth numerous times, delivering wicked ogresses, sorceresses, and other children with faces only a mother could love. Through these births, Loki became the foremother of all magical women. The learning was complete, the time was over, and Loki then returned to being a man.

Another time, Loki took on the form of a maiden and resided under the earth in the land of the dead. For eight years, she lived as a witch who was also a milkmaid—even witches need day jobs! Loki again became pregnant and bore many other witches. Loki loved the number eight, and she gave birth to one witch each winter for those eight years.

Loki also explored their identity during one of the most significant moments in the lives of all the Norse gods. The gods ordered a wall built around Asgard to prevent invaders from reaching their kingdom, and they promised the builder all sorts of treasures and prizes if he could complete it in one season without the help of anyone else. The gods themselves were being tricky and made this deal thinking they could get the wall built at no cost, assuming the builder could not do it in time and they therefore wouldn't have to pay.

However, the builder recruited Svadilfari, the most well-known and smartest stallion ever. The gods sought Loki's help to sabotage the builder. Loki transformed into a mare. When the mare met Svadilfari, the pair of horses immediately fell in love and ran away together. Svadilfari abandoned the work that the builder was to do, leaving the wall unfinished.

In her mare form, Loki was truly in love with Svadilfari. Over time she became pregnant and gave birth to an eight-legged horse—still a fan of the number eight—that they named Sleipnir. Sleipnir grew to become the most well-known, fiercest horse, joining Odin—king of the gods—in countless battles. Sleipnir possessed the magical power to journey to the realm of the dead, where Odin frequently battled to maintain his power.

Despite all the help Loki provided, he still was misunderstood for his queerness. As the end of the world approached, Odin called Loki an agr, a terrible Old Norse insult about Loki's gender and sexuality. Everyone knew about his time as the mare and the fact that Loki was mother to Sleipnir. But Odin also told everyone of Loki's years as the milkmaid and of the countless children the god of mischief had birthed, in order to shame Loki, as all things associated with the feminine were inferior. Loki could never understand the homophobia, transphobia, and misogyny of Odin and the other gods.

Regardless of the offense, Loki chose not to dispute what Odin said. Loki wanted the world's definitions to change and loosen. Loki knew that denying or fighting back simply reinforced beliefs that were already far too rigid. So Loki stood by who he was, in all his many fluid parts. Loki continued to take on the shape or form of whatever he needed to—maiden, witch, mare, handsome man, elder, youth—standing firm in his queer and fluid identity, fighting for the world to open just a bit more with each push.

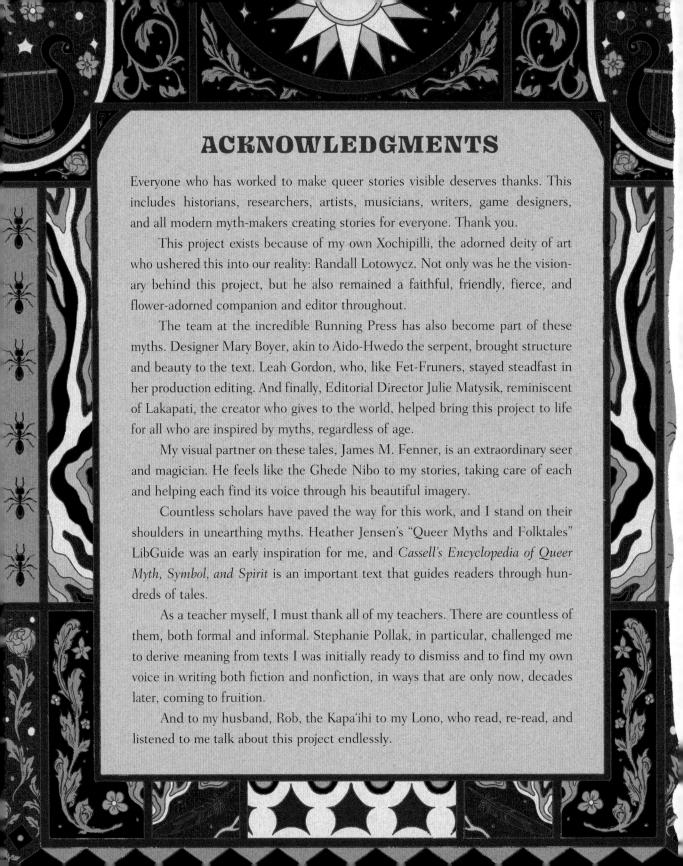

ACKNOWLEDGMENTS

Everyone who has worked to make queer stories visible deserves thanks. This includes historians, researchers, artists, musicians, writers, game designers, and all modern myth-makers creating stories for everyone. Thank you.

This project exists because of my own Xochipilli, the adorned deity of art who ushered this into our reality: Randall Lotowycz. Not only was he the visionary behind this project, but he also remained a faithful, friendly, fierce, and flower-adorned companion and editor throughout.

The team at the incredible Running Press has also become part of these myths. Designer Mary Boyer, akin to Aido-Hwedo the serpent, brought structure and beauty to the text. Leah Gordon, who, like Fet-Fruners, stayed steadfast in her production editing. And finally, Editorial Director Julie Matysik, reminiscent of Lakapati, the creator who gives to the world, helped bring this project to life for all who are inspired by myths, regardless of age.

My visual partner on these tales, James M. Fenner, is an extraordinary seer and magician. He feels like the Ghede Nibo to my stories, taking care of each and helping each find its voice through his beautiful imagery.

Countless scholars have paved the way for this work, and I stand on their shoulders in unearthing myths. Heather Jensen's "Queer Myths and Folktales" LibGuide was an early inspiration for me, and *Cassell's Encyclopedia of Queer Myth, Symbol, and Spirit* is an important text that guides readers through hundreds of tales.

As a teacher myself, I must thank all of my teachers. There are countless of them, both formal and informal. Stephanie Pollak, in particular, challenged me to derive meaning from texts I was initially ready to dismiss and to find my own voice in writing both fiction and nonfiction, in ways that are only now, decades later, coming to fruition.

And to my husband, Rob, the Kapaʻihi to my Lono, who read, re-read, and listened to me talk about this project endlessly.